Acknowledgements:

Editing: Lori White Creative Editing Services

Cover Design: Dar Albert, Wicked Smart Designs

Proofreader: Melinda Kaye Brandt

 Created with Vellum

PHANTOM FIRE

A SMALL TOWN SURPRISE BABY DRAGON SHIFTER ROMANCE

WINGED WARRIOR

DELTA JAMES

For Chris, Renee, and the Girls:
Who make my life so much easier and better
And
For My Readers who make
all the good things in my life possible

Thank you!

KEEP UP WITH DELTA ON SOCIAL MEDIA

Facebook page
Facebook group
Instagram
TikTok
Bookbub
Goodreads
Patreon

Signup for my newsletter and
Get the good stuff...
Each month Delta shares her writing updates, novel releases, exclusive content and some fun personal stories.
Plus - there's often a giveaway!

Thank you!

PROLOGUE

In the Age of Dragons, the immortal beasts ruled the skies and the land below. When the Age of Man arose, the prophets foretold of a time when dragons would be no more. Desperate to ensure their viability, they chose a great sorcerer to help them save their kind, but magic always has a price.

The strongest warrior from each of the ruling clans retained their immortality as well as being granted life as a human-dragon shifter. Those twelve banded together to form the Phantom Fire—elite warriors and mercenaries who would ensure the survival of their kind.

But in exchange for this boon, magic demanded an even greater sacrifice—the warriors were condemned to live without a mate until they were willing to give up their immortality for their eternal flame.

CHAPTER 1

FALKOR

*W*ind River Mountains
Continental Divide
Wyoming, United States
Three Months Ago

The "Winds," as they were called, were the most remote mountain range in the lower forty-eight states of America. They had been the home of the Phantom Fire long before the North American Continent had even stopped evolving. On the edge of one of the great precipices, Falkor stood alone, breathing in the frigid air before allowing himself to lean over the edge into a freefall until spreading his wings, he caught the wind and soared up among the clouds.

They were to lose another of their number this day. Brososs had been blessed to find his eternal flame. She was human and had undergone the transition. As was their way, Brososs would sire his own replacement and when the boy came of age, he would take his father's place among the brotherhood —the band of elite warriors known as the Phantom Fire.

Soaring high above the clouds, looking down onto the rugged landscape below, Falkor thought back to all the initiation and departure ceremonies he had borne witness to. He alone had been there from the beginning. He was the last of the original twelve warriors—those who chose to live separate and apart from the rest of their kind in order to ensure the dragons' survival.

"Falkor," intoned Ageor. *"You have chosen the immortal life of the warrior. From this time forth you will live alone with only your brothers as family. You will forsake the comfort of a mate until such time as you are gifted with an eternal flame. Then and only then, will you forsake your immortality, and live as a mortal dragon-shifter."*

"I will hold to that vow," answered Falkor.

"You will leave your clan and cleave only to those of your brotherhood for the protection and continuation of your kind. No longer will your birth clan take precedence in your favor. Your new clan, your only clan, will be that of the Phantom Fire."

"To that I will hold."

"Those chosen from the Origin of Twelve will always comprise the Phantom Fire. Only when you are united with your eternal flame will you be released from your sacred vow, but the

price of that boon will be to sire the one who will pick up the mantle for your clan in memory of those who have gone before."

"And to that I will hold."

Falkor was of royal blood, brother to Zafira, one of the doomed warrior queens who had given her life to try and defeat the Cherufe, the mortal enemies of all—dragon, shifter, and human alike. He had been chosen to lead the Phantom Fire all those millennia ago. It had been a long and sometimes lonely existence.

How had he thought any of that would be easy? He smiled to himself. Being alpha to a group of warriors was not for the faint of heart. But he was proud to say no member of the brotherhood had been banished. Throughout the ages, some had been fortunate enough to find their eternal flame, leave the brotherhood, and forge a new life for themselves. And each time they had sired their own replacements. He now led dragon-shifters who were many times removed from those with whom he had originally joined.

So deep in his thoughts was Falkor, that he failed to notice their newest recruit climbing up through the clouds to join him. To cover his own lapse and to teach the boy a lesson, Falkor folded his wings and dove at Nadon in an aggressive maneuver, tagging Nadon's wing and sending the young dragon in a death spiral toward the earth.

Under Falkor's watchful eye, Nadon managed to

control his panic and pull out of the fatal spin, spreading his wings and flapping them slowly to stabilize himself, but remain within the shadow of the more powerful dragon lord.

Falkor glided down to join him. "Well done. I thought I might have to come down to save you, but you recovered nicely. Remember that not all dragons are our brothers. The fact is we have some rather nasty enemies. Tis best never to startle a dragon, unless you mean to attack him, and in that case, try not to make so much noise and come from above, not below."

"Yes, Falkor. I mean Alpha…"

"Falkor will suffice. While I am alpha to the Phantom Fire, we are each bound to the same vows and to each other. Our hierarchy is far less rigid. I knew your sire, Emron, well. I called him friend as well as brother."

"Like Brososs?"

"Very much so. I will miss the one who leaves us today but will celebrate with him his joining with his eternal flame."

"Does it ever bother you that after all these years, your eternal flame has not joined with you?"

"I will not say I would not have welcomed her to my life, but I think Ageor knew our kind well and knew that our intelligence and common sense could often be overruled when we breathed in the scent of a drakaina. There is nothing quite so sweet, intoxicating, and arousing as the smell of a drakaina who is ripe and ready for fucking. It is only our vows that bind us to one another that allow us to sacrifice the pleasure of their wet heat and fulfill our mission."

"So, until our eternal flame presents herself, we live celibate?" asked Nadon, the last word coming out in more of the high-pitched squeak of the young than the deeper timbre of a dragon lord.

Falkor chuckled—the sound rumbling up from deep within him. "We're dragons, boy, not monks."

"Sobek asked if you could join us and sent me to find you."

"Which you have done. Go and tell him I shall be down shortly."

Falkor banked away from Nadon and began to climb back into the skies—his thoughts returning to darker themes and images of days gone by.

Banished by their own kind, the elite fighters of the Phantom Fire were called in to settle disputes and to deal with things many clans had forgotten how to do for themselves. Their skills as champions of battle had made them rich, and their treasure was hidden deep within the Winds, untouched by time, man, or dragon.

There had been a time when the peaks they inhabited had been considered too remote, too rugged, and too wild to be traversed on foot, horseback, or vehicle. What little entertainment the Phantom Fire allowed themselves was usually at the expense of some poor soul who thought he'd be among those brave enough to try and conquer the harsh terrain.

The skies above the clouds were blue and cold and snow was beginning to make its appearance on the lower levels of the mountains. He flew among the clouds, small droplets of ice sizzling along his wings as soon as they landed. One of the nicer things about being a dragon was the ability to regulate one's temperature. Unfortunately, the ability didn't survive the shift; but still, it could prove handy.

He dipped below the clouds and flew close to the surface of the Wind River, for which their mountain range was named. Falkor dipped a wing in the white-capped current of the river and then soared up into the clouds to try and clear his head. Melancholy had been his companion for the last several hundred years, but rumors were rife that the Cherufe were returning. Falkor knew he would have to shake it off in order to lead his warriors in the fight.

Even if the legends were wrong and his sister, Zafira didn't return, the Phantom Fire would be needed. He was the only one who had been there the first time around.

Falkor spiraled down out of the sky, finding a place on a large rock bathed in sunlight to land and shift. The sun's heat felt good on his old bones— heavy emphasis on "old." He sprawled naked on the rock, enjoying the way the sunlight warmed his skin while the cool breeze raised goosebumps along it.

He didn't tarry long, knowing full well that a naked man in the Wind River Mountains would draw attention to the area in which they had their home, which was the last thing any of them wanted. Falkor shifted again, returning to his dragon form and taking to the skies, using the clouds for cover until he could drift down and land within the hidden stronghold of the Phantom Fire. They had held this high valley in the Wind River Mountains since before the beginning of recorded time. As man had expanded their dominion, the Phantom Fire had acquired and recorded their ownership of their holding, hiding it and themselves away from prying eyes.

Once inside his dwelling, Falkor stood under the shower, thinking the ability to bathe inside under water whose temperature could be regulated might be one of the finest inventions in the last several centuries. Donning his clothing, Falkor emerged from his home, joining the others in the common area.

"Someone needs to go," said Nadon to Sobek, beta to the Phantom Fire.

"It isn't that I don't agree with you, boy. I just don't agree that it should be you," replied Sobek.

"I'm not a prisoner here, and no one told me I was going to have to do without the pleasures of being with females," argued the younger dragon.

"Problem?" asked Falkor as he joined them.

"Nadon says the Sierra Club is having a big fundraiser and is going to reveal some of their plans for next year. Apparently, there's a group who wants to see if they can't make use of the Winds to turn a profit. The Sierra Club is fighting them."

"I think one of us should be there, Alpha."

"Specifically, he thinks it should be him, and mainly because he wants a trip to Boulder so he can get laid."

"It's been a while."

Falkor laughed. "The last time I got laid you weren't even born."

All the color drained out of Nadon's face.

"He's joking, lad," Sobek assured him, "although not by much." He turned to Falkor. "He's right, though. You should go. If they're really going to try to commercialize our home, we need to know about it."

"I said I could go. You can't stop me," said Nadon a bit too stridently for Falkor's liking. The young dragon needed to learn that while their hierarchy of the Phantom Fire was flatter and less rigid than in a lot of clans, he was still speaking to ranked members of their brotherhood.

"That's your dick talking," said Falkor in a brusque voice. "You're right; you are no prisoner, and you can return to your father's home, but I would point out that you would be the first member of the Phantom Fire to leave the brotherhood in the absence of his eternal flame, and you would bring shame upon your father and your family. You would also be hunted down and killed. But if you getting laid is more important than that, own what you're doing and why. Don't dress it up in trying to do some kind of reconnaissance."

Nadon looked appropriately shamefaced. "You're right, Alpha. My apologies. I'm having trouble adjusting."

Falkor laid his hand on the young dragon's shoulder. "The Phantom Fire is not an easy calling. We are the best-trained and most elite warriors in the world, but it takes its toll. We have a friend at the Sierra Club. I'll see if I can't get an invitation to the fundraiser." Falkor strapped on his sword belt. "Let's go wish our brother well."

The three dragon lords headed for the high altar at the base of a waterfall just outside their camp. The camp itself had long been hidden away, but as modern technology had taken hold and man had ventured into the skies, they had used some residual magic given to them by the descendants of the sorcerer to ensure it could not be seen.

Brososs stood with his eternal flame in front of Zahran, their healer and shaman. Zahran raised his arms.

"Do you, Brososs, choose to forsake the immortal life and leave the brotherhood of the Phantom Fire?"

"I do. I choose to cleave to my eternal flame and share a single lifetime with her and pledge our firstborn son to take my place among those who I have long called brother, as have all my ancestors before me. I leave my immortality behind and begin anew as a mortal." He turned to the drakaina who stood with her hands entwined with his. "Blood of my blood, will you bind yourself to me?"

"I will," she answered, her smile outshining the sun high in the sky in its radiance and warmth.

"Then it is done," said Zahran.

From the edge of the gathering, Sobek stood next to Falkor. "He will be missed," said Sobek.

"As will we all when it is our time to choose a mortal life with our eternal flame. But each of us will pledge a son to take our place and pick up the mantle of the Phantom Fire."

Sobek placed his hand on Falkor's shoulder. "No one could ever take your place, Alpha. Perhaps it is time the Phantom Fire found another way."

Falkor shook his head. "There is no other way. No dragon can serve two masters—either we are solely committed to the Phantom Fire, or we choose to give up our immortality to spend a mortal life with our eternal flame."

"And which would you choose?"

Falkor looked at the man who had stood at his side for more than a thousand years. "That choice has never been thrust upon me and truly I do not know whether I would follow honor or my heart."

Saying nothing more, Falkor left Sobek and went

to congratulate the departing warrior and his bride, pondering Sobek's question far more deeply than he ever had before. Combined with the nightmares of seeing his sister dive into the Rift, he had begun to see a golden-haired woman with green eyes. Could the powers that be at last see fit to balance his great loss with the greatest of gifts?

CHAPTER 2

KESSILY

"So, Mr. Baker, can you explain to the court how it is that you managed to *accidentally* start drilling in an area of pristine wilderness…"

"I don't know that I'd call it 'pristine,'" interrupted Grant Baker, the head of a small-time mining operation as he glared at his lawyer.

Kessily Campbell smiled. The outcome of this trial had been a foregone conclusion the second Baker had entered the courtroom with Alan Messing as his attorney.

"Then what would you call an untouched area of wilderness? An area so remote that had not one of your employees blown a whistle on your illegal operations, you might have gotten away with it?"

"Ungrateful pencil neck," snarled Baker, and still Messing said nothing.

Kessily couldn't decide whether or not Messing

was an even worse lawyer than she'd thought, or whether he disliked his client so intensely that he was willing to let him hang himself. Given that Messing was no friend of the Sierra Club or anyone else interested in protecting the environment, it was more than likely he really was that bad of an attorney.

"An ungrateful pencil neck who you fired in violation of the laws regarding whistle blowers…"

Messing finally got to his feet. "Objection, Your Honor, Ms. Campbell cannot introduce that information into this trial."

"But your client responded and, therefore, opened the door to this line of questioning, or at least as to how the Sierra Club was alerted and how Mr. Baker violated the whistleblower laws."

"Thin ice, Ms. Campbell, leave it alone, but I won't have it stricken from the record or ask the jury to disregard the testimony," said the judge.

"But Your Honor…"

"That's enough, Messing. Your objection is noted, but you let your client get baited into a trap. Be thankful I'm shutting down further questions about your client's violations of all kinds of federal law. The land is owned by the government, is it not, Ms. Campbell?"

"No, Your Honor; the parcel on which Mr. Baker was illegally drilling was immediately adjacent to a small state park, but studies show they were drilling for oil and other minerals that would have rightfully belonged to the State of Colorado."

That had gone better than she thought. The judge had allowed her to get information to the jury that would be damning to Messing's client without even having to lead Baker around to admitting it.

Kessily glanced at the jury and hid her smile. They were outraged. Some of them might be pro-drilling, but they weren't pro-drilling in state or federal parks. She looked at Messing—not only did she know the trial was over, but so did he.

"Your Honor, I'd like to confer with my client before he continues. As we are so close to lunch, might I ask for a recess until one thirty?" asked Messing.

The judge looked at the clock that ticked relentlessly like a metronome and nodded. "Unless Ms. Campbell has an objection?"

"Not at all, Your Honor. I am always happy to accommodate the court and my colleagues."

The judge brought down his gavel with a sharp rap on the bench. "Court is adjourned until one-thirty."

"All rise," said the bailiff as the judge pushed back from the bench.

When the judge had left the courtroom, Messing approached her. "I need a few minutes to confer with my client, and then I'd like a chance to meet with you to propose an offer of settlement."

"Of course, Alan. As I said, I'm always happy to help."

Messing snorted. "Yeah, help my client into a huge fine and enormous settlements with both the whistleblower and the Sierra Club."

"There's an easy way for your client to avoid that kind of thing…"

"Yeah? How?"

Kessily buckled her messenger bag briefcase closed and pulled the strap over her shoulder. "Quit violating the law. I'll be at the White Dove if you want to talk about reasonable settlements. Otherwise," she said, leaning in closer to Messing, "I'll eat your client as a tasty snack on the witness stand."

She spun on her Louboutin heel and headed out of the courtroom, her French-braided ponytail swinging along her spine. God, she loved it when she had the opposition by the short hairs. It had been a bit slow going in the beginning, but Baker had thought he was smarter than all of them—his lawyer, the judge, and her. She wasn't sure about his lawyer, but he had woefully underestimated both her and the judge.

The White Dove was a small café next door to the courthouse. It only served attorneys and courtroom personnel. It provided a safe haven during a trial for those involved in the administration of justice. Kessily was feeling pretty good about where she'd put Messing and his client. It wasn't time to call the Sierra

Club, who was technically her client, or the man who had blown the whistle on Baker. It might not be time to celebrate with a peach margarita—on the rocks, no salt—but certainly a salted caramel shake wouldn't go amiss. The White Dove's milkshakes were to die for. Yeah, a salted caramel shake and a double cheeseburger sounded just right. She'd worry about her diet tomorrow.

The press was being held back from crowding the sidewalk by a permanently installed railing that allowed patrons of the courthouse to come and go at the café without having to muscle their way inside. Kessily entered the White Dove and was hailed by Libby Grafton, who was the owner and chef.

"Hey, Kess! I heard just when you started to put the screws to Baker, Messing asked for a recess."

Kessily smiled. "You know I don't comment on ongoing litigation, but I thought I might have a double cheeseburger and a salted caramel shake…"

"Not that you're celebrating," called Libby.

"Not at all," Kessily responded, finding a small table at the back. The waitress brought her a tall glass of cold ice water. "Thanks."

"Sure thing, Ms. Campbell. I think what you're doing to protect the environment is just super. I'm thinking of maybe becoming a lawyer someday."

"I think that's great," she said, handing her a business card. "If you ever want to talk or ask questions, just reach out. I'd be happy to help in any way possible."

"Wow, thanks! Chef has your order, right?"

"Yes, she does." The waitress wandered off and was quickly replaced by Alan Messing trying to nonchalantly slide into the chair opposite her. "Alan?"

"This is all off the record, right?" Kessily nodded. "My client is screwed, and he knows it. Baker is small time, although he doesn't like people to know that. That was a hail Mary gamble to try and save his company." He passed her a piece of paper. "That's all he has. He showed me his bank records and that of his company. It's legit, Kessily."

She looked at the figure written down. If it was legit, Baker was in worse financial shape than she thought.

"Double it."

"He doesn't have it…"

"He'd have a lot more of it if you refunded him the part of the retainer you haven't used, and given your performance over the past few days, I would think it would put a sizeable chunk into the pot. I think the whistleblower would settle for seventy-five percent up front, a promissory note for the balance, and a glowing reference and recommendation."

Messing looked at her face, assessing his chances of getting a better offer. Seeing none, he asked, "And the Colorado chapter of the Sierra Club?"

"He ceases any and all operations in the state; he

restores the wilderness he destroyed, and we want an account of all oil and minerals he illegally obtained. He sells them on the open market and the net proceeds go to the Sierra Club."

"He won't make a dime," Messing blustered.

"Tell him we aren't asking for gross proceeds, and he will submit to a forensic accounting. In addition…"

"There's more?" gulped Messing.

Kessily nodded. "He tells us who it is that's behind all of these small timers. We want the name of the man behind the curtain."

"You don't know…"

"Oh, but I do. He either gives us the name of whoever it is that's pulling all the strings, or we'll pursue him into bankruptcy and see that other charges are filed. Take it or leave it, Alan, there is no negotiation."

Alan Messing sat back. "You really are a ball-busting bitch, aren't you?"

"Why, Alan," she said in her syrupiest voice, "you do say the sweetest things."

"Give me a minute." Alan stepped away, returning a few minutes later just as her cheeseburger and shake were delivered.

"Don't bother sitting down, Alan. Yes or no? If it's yes, you do the paperwork and have it to my office before five. If not, see you in court."

"He's furious. He called you all kinds of things I never would, and I don't like you very much. I told him his chances of prevailing were pretty much slim to none. He doesn't like it, but you have a deal."

"You can tell the judge we have a deal. I want the dismissal paperwork, the settlement documents, and the money to my office by the end of the day."

"He can only get the amount we offered by the end of the day."

"Then write the dismissal for the day after we get it. We won't sign anything until we have the money. Now go away; my lunch is getting cold."

Kessily finished her lunch and returned to the courtroom where the judge accepted their deal, thanked the jury for their service and dismissed everyone. Kessily walked down the hall and managed to snag the attorney-only elevator to take her down to the secure parking lot. Ever since an unhappy defendant had gunned down opposing counsel as they were headed for their cars, the courthouse had taken steps to protect judges, attorneys, and staff.

She got in her car, started the engine and was just buckling her seatbelt when her phone rang. It was Clancy Carmichael, her boss.

"Yo, Clancy, what's up?"

"You tell me. That bastard Baker called over here complaining about you. As pissed as he was, I'm assuming that you put the screws to him and got what we wanted."

"I don't have it yet, but the deal is predicated on it."

"Damn, girl. I knew you could do it. I have to tell you the national organization was watching this one. They didn't think you could push old Baker into the corner so far, he'd give up the real bastards behind this. I have it on good authority that there is a very real possibility that not only will our chapter be put up for accommodation, but that you will be singled out and may even be on track for attorney of the year."

"Seriously?" she asked, somewhat surprised.

"As a heart attack. You're doing a great job, Kessily. Why don't you take the rest of the week off without using your paid time off and when you come back, we'll talk about you taking on the chief counsel position for the chapter."

She'd been waiting for them to post the opening. She knew that Monica Kent would be stepping down before the end of the year. Her husband had been diagnosed with terminal cancer, and she wanted to spend time with him.

"That would be amazing—both the vacation and the job. I won't let you down."

"I don't think there's anyone who doubts that. You're the right person to take over and were Monica's recommendation."

"Thank you. I'll see you Monday."

"Have a great time and try to do something fun just for you. We've got a lot of work ahead of us."

The call ended and Kessily squeezed the steering wheel, bouncing in her seat. "Yes! Yes! Yes!"

Pulling out of the parking lot, she headed for home. Home. It had been thus until she'd left for Dartmouth. After law school, she'd been recruited by a high-powered law firm in D.C., and she'd considered it. The compensation package was staggering. She'd be able to pay back her student loans in record time. But then the Sierra Club had come calling.

The head of legal affairs for the national chapter had been blunt—they couldn't compete with the other offer in terms of money and perks, but what they could do was offer her a paid position to help save the world. It hadn't taken her but a fraction of a second to pick up the phone and politely decline the first law firm's offer.

She was headed for the home she shared with her mother. When Kessily had returned, it had been intended as a temporary arrangement, but they found as adults they got along much better than they had when Kessily was younger, and with the house set-up in a U-shape with the primary bedroom and ensuite on one side and two spacious bedrooms and a bath on the other, they each had their own side with a common living room/dining room on one side and kitchen/den on the other.

Her mother had her bridge games and her service league and Kessily had her work. Kessily readily agreed whenever her mother told her she sucked at work/life balance, but Kessily didn't really care—she loved her life. But she meant to make the most of the unexpected vacation. She would rearrange and paint her bedroom, buy herself a new bed and mattress and then take a few days for a solo backpack trip into the Wind River Mountains.

The Winds were among the most remote and beautiful mountains and meadows in the world. This was the trip she'd been promising herself ever since she moved back to Colorado, and she meant to enjoy herself.

Maybe she'd see that dragon a man had sworn he'd seen a couple of years ago—not that she believed in dragons, but there was still a part of her that believed anything was possible. And if so, maybe she'd look up to find a dragon soaring among the clouds.

CHAPTER 3

KESSILY

It was a seven-hour drive from her home in Denver to the Wind River Mountain Range up in Wyoming. Sure, there were places to hike or camp much closer to home, but the Winds had always called to her. In Kessily's opinion, their grandeur and remoteness were beyond compare. There were mountain ranges that were taller or were more celebrated, but they were also far more populated and at the moment, the last thing Kessily wanted was people.

Ever since Grant Baker had allegedly killed himself, Kessily had been inundated with press people all vying to get her side of the story. The problem was, she didn't believe Baker was dead, much less had killed himself. No. What she suspected was that he had vast sums of money stashed offshore under an alias, and when it looked like he was going to lose it all, he staged his own suicide and disappeared.

The other alternative was that whoever was behind whatever Baker was involved with had murdered him before he could reveal their identity.

In either event, Kessily had nothing to say on the matter, and Baker was no innocent in what had happened, so she found it hard to feel much sympathy for him. For the family he'd left behind, absolutely, but she never doubted for a minute Baker knew exactly what he was risking when he had done what he did.

Parking her Jeep at the trailhead, Kessily got her backpack out, locked the Jeep, and zipped the keys in the inside pocket of her down vest. Hoisting the backpack into place, she secured it and headed out onto the trail. The fact that there had been only one other vehicle parked in the lot was good news as it meant she should have the solitude she craved.

The fact that it had stick figures on the back windshield indicating a child, a toddler, a baby, and two parents meant that most likely there would be a lot of noise from the little ones. It wasn't that she didn't like children; she did. But right now, peace and quiet was what she was looking for and three little kids enjoying the great outdoors wasn't likely going to produce that. In addition, the Winds offered even experienced hikers a real challenge. She wondered at the wisdom of taking small children on such a difficult hike.

Kessily caught sight of them as she approached

the first fork in the trail. She almost felt sorry for the parents—almost. From the set of their backpacks, they didn't seem to be experienced hikers. In addition, the father had the baby in a sling around his front, the mother was trying to wrangle the toddler by keeping hold of his hand, and the little boy, who appeared to be six or seven, was running around ignoring his parents. The Winds were no place for inexperienced hikers, much less inexperienced ones with small children in tow.

Approaching them, Kessily called, "Can I be of help?"

The father looked embarrassed.

"Yes, please," answered the mother, looking relieved.

Kessily joined them and put down her own pack, leaning it up against a tree. She went to the mother and tried to adjust her pack. She could make adjustments, but it wouldn't do much good to fix the problem. Glancing at the father's backpack, Kessily realized it, too, appeared to be packed improperly, and he was off balance. Add a baby to that, and the best that would happen was that he would end up with a sore back.

"Um, I don't mean to be butting into your business, but can I ask who packed your backpacks? I can help with adjusting the packs, but they don't appear to be packed properly, which is going to make hiking a whole lot more difficult."

"We're pretty inexperienced," admitted the mother. "In fact, this is my first time and only my husband's second."

Kessily hoped her face didn't betray her shock. The Winds were not a casual hike or camping trip. They were considered to be among the most challenging in North America by experienced hikers. What these two neophytes with three small children were thinking when they'd decided to head out was completely beyond her.

Instead of telling them she thought they were way in over their heads and idiots for trying, she said, "Well, how about we take the packs off, and we'll see if we can't make them more balanced and easier to use."

"You wouldn't mind?" the young mother asked. "I mean, yours look so much neater."

Kessily nodded. "I've been backpacking most of my life, and I'd be happy to help."

"Only if you're sure you know what you're doing," said the father.

Biting her tongue to avoid giving him a scathing reply, Kessily smiled. "As I said, I've been hiking, backpacking, and camping most of my life, and the Winds are among my favorite ranges in the world. They're so challenging and really test your abilities and endurance."

Kessily took the mother's pack so she could wrangle the toddler and the little boy and then helped the father with his backpack and the baby, giving the baby back as quickly as she could. It wasn't that she didn't like children, but having been diagnosed with PCOS, she didn't think motherhood was in the cards for her.

She tried telling herself she'd never had any burning desire to be a mother, but ever since the doctor had told her that he suspected and then confirmed the PCOS diagnosis, every time she held a baby, she could hear the tick, tick, tick of her biological clock. She compensated by working harder and giving herself little time to think about it. Her mother had been incredibly supportive and encouraged her, if she really wanted to be a mother, to consider adoption, but not knowing if she wanted to even raise a child, she hadn't given it much thought.

Kessily began removing the items in the family's backpack. What she found left her fuming.

"I noticed when I was helping you that the pack seemed very different in weight…"

"That's because I had to carry the baby," said the father defensively.

Kessily was beginning to believe the father was a douchebag. He wanted to hike the Winds—there was a certain romance and panache to doing so—but he had almost no experience, his wife had none and there were three young children.

"I understand that, but did you know they actually make backpacks that will safely carry a baby?"

"They are way overpriced, and they don't carry much at all…"

"Except the baby." Kessily knelt down and began redistributing the items by weight. "And having two small children to watch, the Winds wouldn't be my pick. There are places here that are dangerous for an adult, much less a kid." She let that sink in. "Okay, so here's kind of the rule of thumb for packing a backpack. At the bottom, you put softer items: sleeping bag, clothing, sleeping pad, and your pillow. In the core section, you put your food, water, tent, and camp stove. Do you have bear canisters and cable for securing your food? This is bear country. On top, you put bear spray, snacks, first aid supplies, rain gear, and a bathroom kit."

"Um, we don't have some of those things," said the husband who was suddenly realizing he might have made a bad choice.

"I noticed. I'm not telling you what to do, but I don't think you're prepared for the Winds, and I think you have vastly underrated their degree of difficulty."

"Neither of us grew up in families that were into the outdoors. We wanted to give our kids this," he indicated the wilderness. "We want them to have what we didn't."

Kessily stood up. "I get that. I really do, but there are easier hikes and you guys might want to get more experience under your belt before you take your kids. There are a lot of great hiking, backpacking, and camping groups that can really help and offer practical demonstrations. You can usually find groups to go with, so you have backup for each other."

"That's probably a better idea, but we live in Nebraska and took the time off..." Now he was starting to sound whiny.

"There are plenty of other things to do close by. You can take a guided car ride through the Winds. There are dude ranches, and some do a kind of hay cart for families with small children, museums that are geared towards kids learning about Native Americans and the Wild West, and you can stay in one of the nearby hotels and just do some shorter walks along the base. There's a great place that has yurts that might be fun for the kids and relaxing for the two of you."

"Do you think we should go back?" asked the wife.

"Of course, she does. She's just trying to be tactful," answered the husband.

"Why don't you give your wife the baby. You and I will repack your backpacks, and you and I can carry one of them between us."

"I don't want to be more of an imposition than we've already been," said the husband.

"You have been nothing of the sort. I am happy to help."

Having repacked the couple's backpacks, Kessily helped him on with his, adjusting the shoulder straps to fit him properly, then pulled on her own. They picked up the third backpack with each of them holding one of the shoulder straps, and then headed back to the trailhead.

Once she had them back in their minivan and headed out in search of tamer adventures, Kessily made her way back up the trail. She'd left in plenty of time to reach one of her favorite places to camp, but she knew she'd have to hustle to get the camp set up before nightfall.

As she'd explained to the young family, the Winds weren't for the faint of heart or for the inexperienced. The Winds were serious mountains that were intent upon keeping their secrets. This was one of her favorites. It led through some gnarly canyons, holes through the rock, steep climbs and shallow ledges. But at the end lay the Cauldron of Fire, so called because it was an almost impenetrable ring of peaks that were formed by volcanic eruptions millions of years ago, and now lay under dense cloud cover. They were thought to be extinct, but every once in a while, there were reports of bursts of flames amidst the deep sound of rolling thunder.

The Cauldron of Fire, or at least the places from which you could see the magnificent mountain tops, was usually a three-day hike. She found a good spot to make camp the first night. She wasn't quite as far along the trail as she wanted to be, but she wasn't too far behind schedule and besides, it was her schedule. She could do as she liked.

The second day began a more serious ascent up into the mountain range. She had to stop and catch her breath, but that, too, was par for the course. She continued on up the steep hiking path, pushing aside any and all thoughts concerning work. She worked hard—too hard according to her mother—so when she wasn't working, she tried not to think of work.

Along about dusk, she had her usual campsite within reach. As she rounded the corner, she realized it was in use. The woman emerging out of the bright orange tent smiled as she spotted Kessily and raised her hand.

"Hello, sister," she called. She was dressed in jeans and a pretty sweater with Native American-inspired artwork intricately woven into the sweater. Her jeans were tucked into traditional moccasins instead of hiking boots.

Kessily looked all around her to see to whom the woman was referring.

The woman laughed. "Yes, I mean you. I've been waiting for you."

"You have? Do we know each other?" Kessily asked as she reached into her pocket for the bear spray—if it could drop a grizzly, surely it could drop a medium-sized female.

"There is no need for violence or confusion. I am known as She Who Listens."

"What do you listen to?" asked Kessily.

"To all the living things. They speak to me."

Curious, Kessily moved closer. "What do they tell you?"

"Many things. For instance, they say you are on a great quest."

Kessily smiled and approached her. There didn't seem to be any reason not to. "I'm hiking up to the Cauldron of Fire."

"Ah, it is the dragon you seek. He searches for you, as well."

Okay, so the woman is a little bit crackers. Perhaps I'll move along and hope she doesn't follow.

"You think I'm not right in the head, but I am. There is a reason you feel at peace when you are within sight of the Cauldron. It is because he is there and has been waiting. He will come to you, and you will bear his child."

"I'm not quite sure how to tell you this," Kessily said, politely, "but it is next to impossible for me to get pregnant. I have something called PCOS. It will prevent me from ever having children."

"Dragon seed is strong. I can prove to you that what I say is true."

"Short of producing a dragon, I don't think that's possible. But you have yourself a nice day."

Kessily turned to leave, and she heard the woman scurrying back into her tent. She didn't think anything good could come of that. She picked up her pace and began to put as much distance between herself and the mad woman as she possibly could. When the sound of the woman exiting her tent and starting after her reached her ears, Kessily broke into a run.

"Wait, sister! I mean you no harm," the woman said as her hand closed around Kessily's upper arm and spun her around. In her hands was a large deck of ornate cards. "Pick one."

"No, thanks. I have friends waiting and want to get to them before they start to worry."

The woman frowned and shook her head. "No, you don't. There is no one who waits for you. Pick a card. Listen to the message the gods send to you, and I will leave you in peace. I am nothing more than their messenger. When you have listened, I will go."

The woman held out the deck of cards, and hesitantly Kessily started to pick one but glanced at the woman's face to see if there was any indication that she wanted her to pick a specific card. There was nothing. This woman would be hard to beat in a poker game. Her expression showed no emotion whatsoever.

"Pick."

Kessily withdrew a card and handed it to the woman, who smiled. "You chose the silver dragon of imagination, possibility, and self-discovery."

Looking at the card, all Kessily could see was a

silver dragon flying high over the peaks of a set of mountains that looked oddly familiar. The sky above it was midnight blue with shining stars that cast their light on the snow-capped peaks.

"What are you trying to tell me?" Kessily asked.

"It is not I who speaks to you, but the dragon lord who will claim you. I wish you well, sister." The woman turned around and returned to her campsite.

Wanting to put as much distance between them as possible, Kessily headed up the trail at a fast pace—just short of running. *What a nut job. Nice enough, but clearly not quite right in the head.*

Kessily rounded the bend and headed up a steep incline. As she reached the top, she paused to catch her breath. The air was getting thinner at this elevation, even for someone born and raised in Colorado. Standing up, she adjusted her pack and looked toward the horizon at her destination—the Cauldron of Fire. In that moment, she realized where she'd seen the mountain peaks depicted on the dragon card.

Shrugging out of her backpack, Kessily hid it behind a large boulder and began to run back down the path to the woman's campsite. She knew this trail like the back of her hand; the campsite was the one she always stayed at. Sprinting the last one hundred yards, she stopped short and stared. She looked around and stared again. Maybe she had missed a turn…?

No, this was the place.

The only problem was, there was nothing there. The site was as empty as if nothing, and no one, had ever been there.

CHAPTER 4

FALKOR

S *nake River Guest House*
Boulder, Colorado
Several Weeks Later

The hotel was alive with environmentalists and philanthropists reacting to the speech and call to arms —so to speak—by the new program director for the club, who'd introduced some of their more well-heeled patrons and volunteers.

When the voluptuous blonde Falkor had been trying without success to ignore all night was acknowledged, she stood and gave a half-hearted wave and a disarming half-smile. She was gorgeous. From the time his attention was drawn to her, he hadn't been able to take his eyes off her. Tall with a curvy figure, and apparently smart. She was a top-notch environmental lawyer out of Denver.

In his opinion, she was sex personified. Her hair hung past her shoulders, tumbling down her back in a cascade of blonde curls that contrasted beautifully with her tanned skin and green eyes. She had curves that called to any man—be he dragon or human. She had many qualities that appealed to him, and he felt his cock stir; something it hadn't done in a long time.

The longer he stared, the more he found to be attracted. The way her short, sequined dress clung to her body left little to his imagination. The scoop neck showed just the right amount of cleavage and dipped down to the small of her back in a sexy plunge. Falkor could easily envision having her naked, his hands on her breasts, suckling at a nipple.

He allowed his eyes to drift back to hers and saw her smiling at him as she lifted her drink in a mock salute, laughing at him... or with him. He left those at his table and made his way over to her.

She held out her hand. "Kessily."

He took her hand as she stood up, enjoying her smooth soft skin. "Falkor. Were you laughing at me, Kessily?"

She headed away from the table to a relatively quiet corner of the large banquet room. "No. It was more that I was laughing with you. This is not your sort of gig, is it?"

"Hardly," he said with a smile. "I thought part of tonight's celebration was about you."

Kessily shook her head and waved him off. "It wasn't that big a deal. I beat a small mining company with a third-rate lawyer."

"My guess is you're selling yourself short and doing so deliberately."

He noticed the dimples in her cheek when she smiled. "Maybe. I scare off a lot of guys."

"You're a deadly combination: beauty, brains, and —my guess—more than a little moxie."

She leaned into him. "Do I scare you, Falkor?"

He slid his hand underneath her silken hair and around the back of her neck, drawing her in. "Not even a little bit."

"Would you like to go up to my room?" she asked breathlessly.

"Only if you're not planning on my leaving until morning."

"Think you can keep up with me all night?" she teased.

"I don't think that'll be a problem."

He grasped her hand and pulled her out of the room, elbowing his way through the crowd until he reached the elevators. He punched the up button— more than once, which caused her laughter to fall around him like the soft shroud of a summer cloud.

The doors opened and he pulled her inside. Another partygoer was about to step in when Kessily pushed the button for her floor and laid her hand on the other man's chest. Falkor felt a spike of arousal and anger surge through his system.

"Take the next one," she said as the doors closed.

Falkor would never be sure if the doors had closed all the way or not before he pushed her back into the wall. Leaning in close enough that his hard thigh was between her legs, and she could feel his cock as it strained against his fly, he said. "I can't remember the last time I was called to a woman the way you call to me. You might regret this or forget it, but I promise you… I never will."

There wasn't even the faintest trace or sign of fear. All he could scent was her arousal mixed with the perfume she was wearing. Her hand traced the line of his jaw and trailed down to his cock where she boldly pressed herself against him.

The elevator stopped, the doors opened, and Kessily used her keycard to gain entry to her room, where she pulled him inside by the lapels on his suit jacket. They came together in a maelstrom of want and need. She was shoving his jacket off his shoulders as he unzipped the back of her dress and let his hand slide inside, cupping her ass, while the other brought her mouth back to his so he could plunge his tongue inside to dance with hers. All the while, the two of them were getting naked as fast as they could without losing any skin-to-skin contact.

Falkor tipped her back on the bed and fell on her

like a thirsty man who'd been denied water for far too long. Kneeling between her legs, he ran his hands from her firm calves up behind her knees to her soft, inner thighs, loving how she moaned in response. Her breathing was labored and fast, just this side of panting.

Drawing one leg up and over his shoulder and spreading her wide, he tongued the entrance of her pussy just deep enough to ensure she was as aroused as he before licking and nibbling his way up to her clit. He swirled his tongue around her swollen nub before latching onto it as he eased two fingers inside her. She was slippery and soft—more than ready and willing.

He began stroking her as she writhed on the bed, her head shaking back and forth as she called his name. Falkor had to wonder if the humans of this time had lost their ability or willingness to please their females. Were she drakaina, she would have long ago been claimed by a warrior strong enough to bring her to heel.

Her body stiffened and she cried out as she gushed her climax onto his hand and he nipped her clit, making her tremble as he licked his way back down to her slit and lapped up all the honey that was there.

"Did that just happen?" she said, sounding far more unsure of herself than she probably wanted to.

"It did," said Falkor, standing and drawing her to

her feet. "And it's going to happen again and again until you cry uncle, or the sun rises. If you want me to go, tell me now. Otherwise, it's *my* turn."

The weeks that had elapsed since his encounter with Kessily had proven to be difficult for Falkor. Never had he longed for any female—human or drakaina— the way he did her. Falkor soared above and through the wispy bits of cloud above the Colorado River. The breathtaking beauty of his home never ceased to speak to a part of his soul he had long thought dead. His sister, Zafira, had returned, just as she had promised to do. Granted, she shared her body and soul with another, but Falkor considered her to be a sister, as well.

Raine/Zafira was now happily mated to her eternal flame.

Falkor watched his sister and the woman with whom she shared both body and soul marry her eternal flame—both the man and the dragon spirit that had saved his life. That they were eternal flames could not be doubted.

Raine had found him sitting alone. He wasn't looking at the celebration below, but at the southern horizon. His face showed neither peace nor contentment.

"A penny for your thoughts," she said as she

joined him and handed him the champagne bottle while she held the glasses.

"I doubt they're worth that… to anybody," he said with a sad smile as he poured the sparkling wine.

"Is there a specific anybody you're brooding about?"

"No, why do you ask?"

"Because Sobek thinks there is."

"Sobek needs to mind his own business."

"I pity betas." Falkor looked at her, sharply. "Really, I do. They have to put up with all your alpha bullshit and you and Cooper snarl at them when all they're trying to do is to ease your burden."

"Now that you're bonded to Cooper, I have no burden. Problem solved."

Raine tipped the champagne bottle over his head, emptying its contents. A bit of it splashed on her gown.

"I'm sending you the cleaning bill," she quipped before he could growl at her.

"Truth is truth."

"What is it?" she asked. "If you want, Zafira can come forward to talk to you."

He placed his hand on hers. "Not necessary. You are every bit as much my sister as she is."

"Then tell me. I can't stand to see you so unhappy when I'm just over-the-moon."

She waited for a moment for him to speak. Falkor wondered how much liquor she'd had to get Sobek to consume to tell her anything at all. The beta to the Phantom Fire was a hard nut to crack.

"What's her name?" Raine prodded gently.

"I am going to kill him," Falkor said evenly.

"Don't. He didn't say anything specifically, and I spent a fortune on vodka trying to get him to talk."

Falkor laughed. "Ah, so that's why he had such a nasty hangover. You are a very naughty drakaina."

"So I'm told on a regular basis. What's her name?"

He shook his head, chuckled, and downed the champagne. "Her name, little sister, is Kessily."

He had returned home after the ceremony unable to stop thinking of Kessily Campbell, the woman with whom he'd shared an intensely passionate night several weeks before. She was a prominent environmental lawyer who had joined the good fight with the Sierra Club to try and block the development of the Winds. Falkor had found it increasingly difficult to dismiss her from his thoughts.

She had been the personification of sex—blonde curls tumbling down her back, skin kissed by the sun as if she'd flown too close to it and deep green eyes that seemed to be from another world. Her curvy figure called to him as no other had ever done, which considering his age, said a lot. She didn't dress to emphasize it, and he wondered idly if she tried to hide her loveliness from the world or just didn't see it for herself.

Falkor had thought to slip out of her hotel room to avoid any awkwardness. She was human and he was dragon, not just any dragon, but the leader of the Phantom Fire. They eschewed all relationships and only left the order to bond with their eternal flame. There was no future to be had with the voluptuous human.

He walked out of the bath to find her kneeling, something he hadn't expected. Her head was bowed submissively, and her thighs spread to show the evidence of her arousal mixed with his dried cum, the scent of her desire permeating the air. Falkor was hard pressed to ever remember a time he'd found a woman so alluring and arousing.

"I know this is a one-time thing, and I want you to know that I have no regrets, save one," she said softly, raising her eyes to gaze into his. It felt like she could read his soul.

"I would prefer you have no regrets, so what is it?" He couldn't tell if he was more suspicious or intrigued.

"To kneel before you, take you in my mouth, and feel your cum race down my throat and into my belly."

Damn. So much for slipping away in the dawn's early light.

Her hand reached up, grasping his hard length that had responded not only to her words, but to her presence. Even before she had spoken, it had known she was near, and that he could have her again if he chose.

Grasping him at the base of his stalk, she began to work

her fist up and down in strong, sure strokes before wrapping her lips around the plum-shaped head.

Perfection.

Knowing he wouldn't be able to last, he steadied her head in his hands and began to stroke—in and out, allowing her to take him deeper with each stroke. Kessily moaned and let him take the lead as she had done throughout the night. The intensity of what he felt was incredible and his head fell back, closing his eyes in response to the pleasure she gave him.

Her hands and mouth worked in perfect harmony to maximize all the sensation that was centered in the lower portion of his torso. As with everything else, she seemed to enjoy the sexual act as well as the intimacy of her service. She teased, fondled, sucked and stroked every inch of his massive cock as well as his dense balls.

As he increased the pace and intensity of his thrusting, she sucked harder and used her tongue to lave affection in the deep V on the underside of his cock. Holding her head, he drove into her mouth—harder, deeper, and faster. Her breathing became erratic, and he could tell he was on the cusp of choking her, but he didn't care. All he wanted was to fuck her mouth until his orgasm overwhelmed him, and he could send a torrent of his cum down into her belly.

His body tensed and he closed his eyes so she couldn't see the ethereal flame that blazed there as he gave himself up to the intensity of his climax. When he was finished, he looked down at her as she sat back on her heels and stared up at him.

"You're the most beautiful man I've ever been with."

"I am far from beautiful, little one. The scars of my life are riddled all across my body."

"Which only show you had the will to survive." She rocked again as she got gracefully to her feet. "Thank you for last night and this. I will treasure the memory."

She'd left him standing there as she walked into the bath. Not knowing what to say or how to respond, he'd gathered up his clothes, donning only his jeans as he left her room and headed for his own, for the first time regretting the legacy of his immortality.

CHAPTER 5

KESSILY

The last couple of months had been unsettling to say the least. The 'Incident in Boulder' as she had come to call what had happened that night, had affected her far more deeply than she'd thought it would. Falkor—although Falkor what, she hadn't a clue—had been clear that it was nothing more than a one-night stand, but it had felt like so much more. She had just come out of the bath hoping, and even half expecting, that he would be there, but he wasn't.

Kessily had told herself it was for the best, but it hadn't felt that way. Her mother had caught her daydreaming on more than one occasion and had made her return to reality. As bad as her waking hours were, she wasn't sure the ones during which she was supposed to be sleeping weren't worse. She could no longer sleep on her back as the memory of being beneath Falkor's strong, muscular body as he thrust his hips, driving his cock deep inside her, practically brought her to orgasm.

On the other hand, she was finding it increasingly difficult to focus for any length of time. It didn't seem to matter where she was or what she was doing, she would find her brain dismissing what was in front of her and returning to the night she'd spent in Falkor's embrace. Concentrating on her legal briefs had become the fodder for her nightmares, only remembering what it had been like with Falkor pushed all other thoughts aside.

It was difficult not to use the shower massage to get herself off every morning, and she was pretty sure she'd worn her vibrator out. Standing under the hot water, she gazed longingly at the hand-held shower-head. No, she was not going to be late because Falkor invaded her imaginings—day and night. She needed to get over it.

Kessily trotted into the kitchen where her mother was fixing breakfast.

"Kiss," her mother requested, proffering her cheek.

Kessily did as requested. "So, what's on your agenda today?"

"Well, after I make sure you have something proper to eat to start your day, I have my meeting with the Service League. We have our annual fundraising event."

"A bake sale, right?" Kessily teased.

"It isn't a bake sale, and you know it. It's a fashion show, and everyone wants you to be in it."

This would be another of the things nagging at her. Well, to be fair, the event and the other women weren't nagging; no, they left that to Kessily's mom,

Kessily laughed, trying not to snort. "Maybe you and all those women who have watched me grow up, but none of those designers wants to have to put something together for the chubby girl."

"Every other member of the committee has at least one daughter walking the runway."

"And at a size two or four, I'm sure they'll look great. But Mom, we both know that I couldn't even get the waist of one of those things around my thigh. Let's not even think about my boobs." Kessily looked down. "Do my boobs look bigger to you?"

Her mother rolled her eyes as she turned out the perfect omelet onto a plate beside a small bowl of fresh fruit and a buttered English muffin. Okay, it wasn't really butter, it was that spray stuff that romance novel cover model had hawked for years.

"Your boobs look like they always do, and they look just fine. In fact, a lot of those dresses would look so much better on you."

Now, it was Kessily's turn to roll her eyes. "Seriously? There is no way even one of my boobs would fit, much less the whole pair."

"If I can get one of the designers excited about using a plus size model, will you do it?"

Believing that the odds of that were slim and none, Kessily agreed.

The old woman. That was another unsettling thing. She hadn't been able to find hide nor hair of her. The campsite had been pristine. It looked as if no one had been there for months. She checked with the park rangers, but no one had seen a woman matching the description Kessily provided, and one ranger was certain he had passed by there right about the time in question. Weird.

Her mother reached out to take her hand. "I wish you'd tell me what's bothering you. You seem so far away. I know we don't have a normal mother/daughter relationship, but who's to say what's normal? Ever since your father left, it's just been the two of us. We used to tell each other everything."

She didn't need her mother worrying about this stuff. Laying her hand over her mother's, Kessily said, "It's fine, Mom."

"No, Kessily, it isn't. Something happened in Boulder. I know it. I can feel it. You've been distant ever since you got back. And your last trip to the Winds seems to have unsettled you somehow. I wish you'd change your mind and start seeing Millie's son. He's crazy about you."

"Well, Millie wouldn't be once she finds out I can't give her grandchildren."

"Is that what this is about? The PCOS? The doctor didn't say you couldn't have kids; he just said it might be difficult. And even if it proves to be true, you have so much more to offer other than your womb."

Kessily laughed. Her mother did have a way with words. "When I was up at the Winds, I met a young family—three kids, Mom; they had three. A little boy about five or six, a toddler and an infant. I'm usually fine with it, but sometimes when I see things like that, or I hear someone from law school just had a baby— or in many cases, another baby—I can not only hear my biological clock ticking, I can hear the gong sounding."

"I'm so sorry, baby. Did something happen in Boulder?"

Kessily tried to hide her shock. Her mother was astute and could usually read her like a book.

Her mother smiled triumphantly. "I knew it. I just knew it. What's his name?"

"That's not important. It was a one-night stand…" Kessily waited for her mother's reaction.

"What?" her mother asked indignantly. "Did you expect me to have a fit of the vapors? For heaven's sake, Kessily, I've known you weren't a virgin for a long, long time. So, what was his name?"

"I'm not telling you." Especially given the fact that all she had was his first name—or was it his last? God, she didn't even know that.

"Whyever not?"

"Because you'd know somebody who knows somebody who could run down the information for you. Like I said, it was a one-night stand. We both agreed it was just that night. I had a great time, in case you wanted to know, but it was never meant to be."

"Tell me how I raised the singularly most unromantic child that ever lived?"

She didn't want to tell her mom that it was because she had watched the way romance had acted like a wrecking ball in her mother's life. Instead, she said, "Just another disappointment in me you'll have to live with."

Her mother shook her arm. "You listen to me. I have never, and I mean never, been disappointed in or with you. You are the one thing I ever did right in my life, and I wonder if your unwillingness to find happiness with a man is because I have fucked up so many relationships."

"You don't fuck them up, Mom. You just have atrocious taste in men."

The silence hung between them, and then her mother grinned. "You're right. It's them, not me."

Kessily laughed. "Absolutely. You're perfect."

"I am rather wonderful, aren't I? After all, I gave birth to you."

Kessily glance at her watch. "Shit. I'm going to be late."

Kessily finished her breakfast, gave her mother

another kiss and then gathered her things. "I should be home on time tonight."

"I'll be close to your office at the meeting of the Service League. Why don't we meet for dinner downtown?"

"Sounds perfect. Thanks for breakfast, and I'll see you then."

Kessily rushed out the door, down the steps and onto the driveway where her Jeep was parked. She inhaled the air and looked skyward—still no dragon as prophesied by the old woman. The sky was cloudy, grayish blue, and it smelled like snow was in the air.

Kessily rushed into the parking lot of the building where the Sierra Club was located. She rode the elevator up to their floor and rushed to her desk. She still didn't have a corner office, but at least she had an actual office, instead of a cubicle. It had a window with a gorgeous view.

She looked up to see her boss standing in the doorway. "What's up?" she asked.

"I know you just got done with a big case, but any chance you'd take on another one? The case itself isn't huge, and it's not even in Colorado. You're licensed to practice in Wyoming, aren't you?"

"I am, and if you think I'm the person for the case, I can pack my bag and be ready to go in an hour."

He grinned. "If only my wife could say that. I know you like to hike and camp in the Winds." She nodded. "Good, then you at least know the area. Some penny-ante mining company is wanting to use a section of Wind River they own rights to and develop it. They have some fancy lawyer out of New York who seems to think they can bully the citizens and local government into allowing them to build a casino, a resort, and a small private airport so their hoity toity customers can fly in direct."

"In other words, they want to rape the land and make a lot of money for their trouble." He nodded. "Not on my watch."

"That's my girl."

Later that day, Kessily was immersed in the new case up in Wyoming and didn't even notice her mother until she sat down in the chair opposite her desk.

"Mom, you're early," she glanced at her watch. "No, as usual, I'm late. Let me save this and shut my computer down. I can pick it back up in the morning."

A very few minutes later they had left her office and headed down to one of their favorite intimate restaurants. It was off the beaten track, and the food was delicious and the prices reasonable.

Once their salads had been served, her mother asked about her day.

"It was good, and my boss asked me to take on another piece of litigation. He says I'm becoming their go to person for litigation, especially where development and mining companies are concerned. I'll probably have to be in Wyoming for a couple of months. Will you be okay?"

"I'm supposed to be the one who looks after you."

"We've always looked after each other. Why don't you plan to come up at least one weekend a month and I'll do the same."

"I'd like that. When do you leave?"

"End of the week."

"Good. Then you can have dinner with Millie's son tomorrow night."

"Okay, but this is the last time and if he gets handsy again, I'm going to punch him in the face."

Her mother grinned. "I would expect no less."

They finished their dinner and the next night she was sitting across from Millie's son thinking not only did her mother owe her one for this, but so did Millie. All she could do was compare him to Falkor and Millie's son came up short in every regard.

She was just finishing her soup, when she felt her stomach beginning to cramp like it did before she had to throw up. "Excuse me," she said making a hasty retreat to the restroom. She only just made it in time to empty the contents of her stomach into the toilet.

I must be coming down with some kind of bug. That's the second time today I've had to puke.

For the remainder of the week, every morning, she was nauseous and had to throw up. This morning after cupping some water from the hotel's spa-like bathroom to rinse her mouth, she wiped at it with a towel while staring into the mirror. She didn't like what she saw there.

Kessily prided herself on being a realist. Better to know what she was dealing with. She knew a lot of people preferred to stick their head in the sand like an ostrich, but the problem with that was it was far easier for people to kick you in the ass.

That night in a fit of frustration and anger, she'd bought an in-home test at a local pharmacy. Squatting over the toilet so as to ensure she didn't contaminate the urine stream, Kessily peed on the stick and then waited for the requisite three minutes.

Looking into the indicator window she saw the one thing she'd never thought she'd see—a plus sign.

Damn!

CHAPTER 6

FALKOR

*K*essily. Her name seemed seared into his brain. He thought he'd managed to tamp the memory down deep in the recesses of the mind. When he closed his eyes at night he could see her again, feel her beneath him as he moved within her or when her lips had wrapped around his cock. It wasn't so much that she'd gone down on him as it was the way she'd done it. Not so much technique—although that had been amazing—as the sweet submission with which she'd done it.

This was not some woman who had gone to her knees to pay homage. Instead, this was a woman who had knelt in front of him to offer a gift—one he'd been only too willing to take.

She had been intriguing from the moment he caught sight of her across a crowded room. She was accomplished, intelligent, and mind-numbingly beautiful. She appeared to be the most intoxicating mix of predator and prey. Falkor imagined that she was normally the former, but in the presence of a dragon, her instinct for survival had kicked in and forced her to acknowledge that she was, in fact, the latter.

Falkor had been drawn to her like a moth to a flame. Something about speaking her name to Raine had brought the memories rushing back to the fore. It was as if he had unleashed some wild beast that wanted to rule over him. She had ignited a fire in his dragon that threatened to burn out of control.

Of course, being with her left me burning for something I could never have imagined. Kessily Campbell was my eternal flame. He had known from the moment he possessed her and had thrust up into her. Thousands of years he had waited and had told himself long ago that he would walk into eternity alone when the world ended. He had long ago accepted that, but then Kessily had arrived and rocked his world in more ways than one.

No one knew, but since his return, he had searched the internet for news of her, combing legal tomes for her triumphs over those who wanted to rape and pillage the land. Flying high above the clouds in the night sky, he had kept watch over her. He told himself over and over that he was keeping watch, keeping her safe, but he knew it wasn't true.

Shortly after their interlude at the Sierra Club

event, he spotted her walking into a restaurant. Nothing to be concerned about, except that a man had met her at the entrance. Placing his hand on the small of her back, he had guided her inside. Falkor remembered the small of her back well. He had been fascinated by the way it flowed into her lovely ass and hips and had pressed his thumbs into it as he pumped her full of his seed. Jealousy and fury had blazed bright within him, and he'd been forced to fly high into the night sky to keep from breathing fire on the man who dared to touch what should be his.

But she wasn't his and never could be. He knew humans had been made drakaina many times over the millennia, but it did not always turn out well for the human. He had raged at the moon, and swooped down through the peaks that surrounded the city. Falkor had been about to descend on the city to deal with the puny male human when he's spotted Kessily out of the corner of his eye. Had he not been so attuned to her presence; he might have missed her. He watched as she left the restaurant alone and been glad. He knew he shouldn't have been. He should have wanted what was best for her and being with him was not it, and yet a small ember of hope was ignited—one which seemed destined to burst into flames.

A few days after seeing Kessily leave the restaurant, Falkor read a note in the Sierra Club's newsletter about Kessily being assigned to a case involving a section of Wind River. There had been an ongoing legal battle between the Sierra Club and the developer who wanted to turn it into a resort and casino. Such a development would destroy the land they were proposing to develop and could easily spread into the surrounding area. The Sierra Club seemed to think it was a small, but important case that could set long-standing precedents.

The club had no way of knowing how very right they were. The problem was that the development company belonged to Warren Sarkany. A dragon with whom Falkor had a bit of history—none of it good. The section of the river in question was at the river's end where it conjoined with two others and was just outside of the Phantom Fire's territory. It had been a long-held dispute among the ruling clans as to whether or not the mercenary band could actually call any place their home—a notion that the Phantom Fire disputed and had defended over the centuries.

Sarkany's clan had been part of those who had searched for silver and gold all over Wyoming and the Dakotas. While few had found success in Wyoming, with their natural affinity for discovering and hoarding gold, Sarkany's ancestors had found their treasure and had dug in to fight any and all who might want to challenge them.

There had been bad blood between Sarkany's clan and the Phantom Fire from the time they first crossed each other's paths. It was no surprise to Falkor that Sarkany was behind this. After all, they were interested in nothing so much as money and seemed to perpetuate the old cliché of dragons loving and hoarding gold.

Falkor could well remember the fight he'd had with Sarkany as a young dragon. It had not ended well for Sarkany.

Looking down at the defeated wyvern, Falkor breathed fire across his head and spine each time the youngster thought to get back to his feet to challenge Falkor again.

"Stay down, boy. I would prefer not to return your charred remains to your family. This stretch of Wind River and the Wind River Range have been the provenance of the Phantom Fire since long before you and yours ever walked the earth, and it will remain so."

"You are a pitiful old dragon, and your men are mercenaries."

"Our brotherhood has existed since the destruction of the Cherufe by the dragon queens. The members of the Phantom Fire all hail from the original twelve clans—something you and yours will never be able to claim."

Sarkany tried to jump to his feet, but one blast of fire directly over his head convinced him of the seriousness of his situation and the deadly adversary he had been foolish enough to challenge.

Falkor backed off. "Take care, boy, and do not let me catch you snooping around our mountains again. There is nothing for you here."

"Whatever treasure it is you're hiding up there in your stronghold will be mine one day."

Falkor shook his head. "You will never begin to understand the secrets and fortunes that we protect at Dragonwyk."

"We'll see. Someday I will take what it is you hold most dear and destroy it in front of your eyes."

"You will never be able to touch what I hold most dear and should you try, you will not survive the encounter."

Falkor had backed away and watched the young wyvern fly away.

"That one will bear watching when he reaches maturity," said Sobek.

"If he lives that long," said Falkor.

But he had taken Sobek's words to heart and had kept an eye both on Sarkany and those who followed him.

Flying over the disputed section of land, Falkor watched as a man poked around the area, a map and surveyor scope and its tripod in hand. He banked north towards Dragonwyk. The brotherhood kept a cache of clothing in various locations close to their home in case they needed it. Landing in the clearing close to one of their outposts, Falkor was able to pick up the bag in his teeth before flapping his great wings and taking to the sky.

The clouds that gave him cover were white and

fluffy and looked like cotton candy from the county fair drifting through the sky. He turned back to the south and found a secluded place among the trees in which to land, shift, and put on his clothes. He emerged from the trees and headed toward the lone individual walking along the stream bed.

"Well, well, well, if it isn't my old friend Falkor."

Falkor snorted. He should have known it would be Sarkany himself. "We were never friends, boy. In fact, you were never even a worthy adversary. From what I have read, not much has changed."

"You're an arrogant bastard, aren't you? That fight was what? Thirty years ago, I wasn't much more than eighteen and you were the legendary alpha of the Phantom Fire." Sarkany shook his head. "You don't look like you've aged even a day."

"Do you not understand the concept of immortality?"

"I don't believe in fairy tales…"

"And yet here we are—two dragons facing each other."

"You're not welcome here."

"Nor are you," returned Falkor. "You will not win this fight with the Sierra Club, and even if you were to somehow prevail in the upcoming litigation, the Phantom Fire would not allow you to destroy the land so close to our home."

"I have hired the best environmental attorney

money can buy. Bruce Chapman will chew up that girl the Sierra Club is sending like she was nothing more than a tasty snack to be served with ketchup."

"I believe your Mr. Chapman has woefully under-estimated Kessily Campbell. She has put a stop to more than one marauding land rapist."

"'Marauding land rapist?'"

Falkor nodded. "The fact that you want to build some godawful casino as a testimony to your god of money and destroy this pristine wilderness is obscene—as are you. I have only four words to say to you: not on my watch."

"Why do you even care? It's not like any of the high rollers we plan to attract are going to go tromping up into your 'pristine wilderness.'" Sarkany said the last two words with a snide tone of voice.

"As I said, not on my watch."

"I'm not afraid of you."

Falkor shook his head. "No, you are far too foolish for that. Heed my warning, boy, you continue this folly at your own risk."

"I'm no boy. I'm almost half a century old. I'm a man—a very wealthy man."

"You're an overgrown lizard with an inferiority complex. You think you're all grown up. I think you've grown past your prime while I'm still in mine. Stand down, Sarkany. You will not win this fight."

"Think not?" he said as a mist of thunder, light-ning, and flashes of color surrounded him.

Falkor snorted and called forth his dragon. Amidst the firestorm that exploded all around him, Falkor rose from the center like the phoenix only not from the ashes, but from the fire itself.

Sarkany roared into the brilliant blue of the sky, and Falkor scored his scales with a devastating stream of fire. Sarkany bellowed his outrage, flapping his wings and lifting off the ground. Falkor was far more adept at both flying and fighting. He lifted off with speed and power, banking up toward the mountain range he called home, turning over on his back in mid-air and breathing fire at the much younger dragon.

Falkor wanted to get them out of the open area and up where their fight could be more easily concealed. Sarkany gave chase—enraged. He flew straight at Falkor, screeching. Falkor was sure he thought the sound was terrifying; it wasn't. He sounded a great deal like a rutting boar who'd been wounded. That wasn't to say that Falkor wasn't keeping an eye on him. Sarkany snapped his jaws, gnashing his teeth before sending a stream of fire Falkor's way.

Sarkany didn't have the breath or firepower to reach his much older opponent. Sarkany flew at Falkor, intent on ending him. It was never meant to be. Falkor soared up and over Sarkany before diving down, tipping Sarkany's wing as he rocketed towards the earth, only to change direction and climb up into the blue, placing the sun directly behind him.

Blinded by the giant orb of gas and fire, Sarkany blew fire—only this time, his weaker stream was met high above the clouds by the far stronger and even more lethal fire coming from deep inside the immortal dragon. Falkor continued to lock fire streams with Sarkany, driving him down into the river.

Falkor landed beside him, placing one clawed foot on Sarkany's neck, holding him down.

"This is the last time I let you walk away, *boy*."

"Next time…"

"If there is a 'next time,' I will end you. Withdraw your permit requests, leave this place, and never return. The Phantom Fire now claims this land and we will kill anyone who tries to take it from us."

Falkor roared his victory into the wilderness before flapping his great wings, flying directly over Sarkany, and then breathing a ring of fire around him.

That ought to teach him.

SARKANY

How had Falkor gotten wind of his plans? How did he know about the lawsuit? And how did he know the name of the opposing counsel? Falkor might be a great warrior, but Sarkany would not be deterred. It probably wasn't possible to buy off the honorable leader of the Phantom Fire. But was there something he valued more than gold—than his own honor?

Sarkany would find out what it was, and when he did, he would take great pleasure in twisting that knife.

CHAPTER 7

KESSILY

*N*ow *what the fuck do I do? Pregnant? How is that even possible?*

Apparently, it was most definitely possible. She'd taken two more at home pregnancy tests and then called her doctor's office and had her run a blood test. After all, only three out of three urine tests had said she was pregnant. The doctor's call confirming her worst fear came far too quickly on her drive home, and her doctor was far too cheery.

Kessily wasn't sure, but she was almost positive that instead of thanking her she just said, 'Oh shit,' as she pulled into the driveway.

What the hell was she going to do? How did she tell her mother? Those she worked with? Well, of the latter, she would need to assure her boss that she was quite capable of handling the trial up in Wyoming. After all, women worked right up to almost their delivery date unless there were problems. Oh God, what if there were problems? What kind of problems could there be?

She couldn't be pregnant. She didn't know how to be pregnant. The fact was, she wasn't even sure she wanted kids. That wasn't completely true. She thought she did, but she had never expected to be able to have them. And what if it turned out she didn't? It wasn't like she could wrap the kid up, take it back to the hospital, and say she wanted a refund. Oh God, what kind of mother even thought things like that?

Didn't it mean she could be a good mother if she knew that kind of thinking was all kinds of wrong? Couldn't her almost panic at her lack of knowledge give her an advantage over some as at least she knew what she didn't know? And maybe, just maybe, the reason she'd told herself she wasn't sure she didn't want children had more to do with fearing she couldn't have them?? She could do this, right?

She had a great role model in her own mother, and she was sure her mother would help. Her mother might be a little taken aback that she was pregnant with no idea how to contact the father, but Kessily had always known she could count on her mother's unconditional love. Renewed strength flowed through her as she realized: she meant to give that to her baby, as well.

Kessily realized she was still sitting in her car

when her mother came out and knocked on the window. "Kessily? Sweetie, are you okay?"

Kessily opened the door. "I'm not sure, but I think so. No. I know so. In fact, I think I have some wonderful news… miraculous even."

"That sounds wonderful. I made shepherd's pie. Come on inside, and you can tell me all about it."

She followed her mother inside, walking to the bedroom she used for a home office first and laying down her briefcase. She moved on to her bedroom where she pulled off her clothes and looked at her body in the mirror—full on and sideways. She didn't look pregnant, did she? She hung up her office attire, glad that long skirts with cowboy boots worked at the Sierra Club, and then pulled on a pair of sweats and Ugg slippers.

"Did you have a hard day?" her mother asked as she joined her in the kitchen/dining area of their home.

"No," she said, shaking her head slightly, "not particularly."

"I think you're working too hard; you're awfully pale."

"I'm not pale, Mom. I'm pregnant." Her mother almost dropped the casserole dish with the shepherd's pie, which would have been a shame as it was one of her favorites, and her mother always did an excellent job with it. "You should know, you're the first person I've told."

Her mother flew across the room, throwing her arms around her and hugging her close. "I'm so happy! Are you happy? You should be happy. This is wonderful news, isn't it?"

Kessily searched her mother's face, and all her fears faded away. Whatever happened, they would face it together, and they would bring up the child she carried in the most loving home any kid could ever have.

"I wasn't sure at first. All I could think was how did this happen?"

"Well, when a man and a woman get together, sometimes he is able to fertilize…"

"Not funny, Mother."

"It doesn't matter how it happened; what matters is that it did. I know they said you could never get pregnant, but here you are. You always were an over-achiever."

Kessily couldn't help but laugh, which, she was sure, was her mother's intention all along.

"Do you think it happened in Boulder?"

"That or I'm the second woman in history to conceive by immaculate conception."

"Don't be impertinent," her mother scolded. "Are you going to try and contact him?"

"I don't know. I just got confirmation of the preg-nancy from the doctor. The problem is, I don't know his last name."

"Would the gala have a list of all who attended?"

"Yes, but some people bought tickets at the door and others did so anonymously, so there's no guarantee his name will be on it. Do you think I should try and track him down and tell him?"

"Don't you?"

"Again, I'm not sure. I don't need child support or anything from him. I kind of thought maybe you and I could raise him or her together…"

Her mother hugged her close. "Of course, we'll raise my grandbaby together. You're going to have to tell your job that you can't go to Wyoming."

"I'll do nothing of the sort. I'm going to Wyoming. The trial shouldn't take that long, and I'd really like to go up against Bruce Chapman. He's one of the best environmental litigators in the business."

"Are you sure about the father? Doesn't he have a right to know?"

Kessily nodded. "Probably, but honestly, I don't know enough about him to know how he feels about kids, or even if I want him in my baby's life. After all, the man who sired me left before I could walk, and I think I turned out okay."

Her mother smiled. "You turned out beautifully. You have exceeded every dream or expectation I ever had for you. You have made me so proud."

Uncertainty twanged, deep inside. "What if when the baby is older, he or she wants to know about the father?"

Her mother shrugged. "We'll answer any questions he or she might have and be honest."

"We're going to tell my kid I was in Boulder having a good time, was feeling a little lonely and a whole lot horny. I met this hunk, he was great in the sack, and 'ta da!" Here you are."

"I think we might want to think about how we might reframe that, but yes. We will be as honest as we can be and will offer an explanation that is age appropriate. And if you're going to Wyoming, I'm going with you."

"Good God, Mother, you don't need to leave everything behind and come to Wyoming."

"I know how you get when you're in a trial. You work too hard and don't get enough sleep or remember to eat. I'll find us a nice Airbnb and you won't be stuck eating restaurant and fast food. I'll bring my quilting and get started on something for the baby. We can turn your home office into a nursery. In fact, I think if we look at your room, we can put your desk in there, don't you think?"

Her mother was in full-on planning mode. Kessily knew she should probably object but couldn't bring herself to do so.

"Once you win the trial—which of course you will do—we can get started on making that the most adorable nursery in the world," her mother continued. "Do you know what colors you'd like to use?"

"Mom. Stop," Kessily laughed. "I just found out

for certain that I was pregnant. We both know decorating and all that stuff is your bailiwick, not mine, so if you want, I will bow to your experience and superior taste."

"Will you really?" Kessily nodded and her mother clapped her hands together. "Then I think maybe something in the green family so it isn't gender specific and he or she can grow into it. What do you think of wainscoting? I've always loved wainscoting. It's so cottagey. Do you have a theme in mind?"

"Can we do a kind of vintage bohemian, like my bedroom?"

"I think that would be wonderful. This is fate. I know it. Just the other day I was shopping with June, and we saw this amazing bronze crib. Just stunning."

"Let's not go overboard, Mom…"

"Why not? Neither of us ever expected you to have a baby. I think we ought to go big or go home, as they say."

"You're going to go way overboard on this aren't you? Should I even bother with a budget?"

"Not unless you want to see how much I blow it. You tell me what you have to spend, and then I'll chip in the rest. You are excited, aren't you?"

"I think so. I'm still just trying to wrap my head around this." Kessily stopped for a moment and bit back a sob.

"You can do this, baby," her mother said, wrapping her arms back around her. "You aren't alone, and whatever happens, this baby will have the most amazing life."

Kessily looked deep into her mother's eyes and felt as though a weight had been lifted from her. Her mother was right. This baby, her child, was going to have a truly wonderful life.

She grinned at her mom, "Okay, let's do this."

Two days later, she met Millie's son for coffee. He'd been calling almost every other day since she'd left him sitting in the restaurant. She smiled and waved as he entered the coffee shop.

"Hi, Hal. Thanks for coming. I wanted to apologize about how I left you…"

"My mom explained that. Are you feeling better? Was it something serious?"

"That's kind of why I wanted to talk to you. I wanted to apologize and let you know I wasn't feeling well, which obviously you heard. I followed up with my doctor, and she confirmed that I'm pregnant."

She let the words hang between them.

"But you're feeling better, right?"

"I am, actually. Thanks for asking. You aren't the father," she said, laughing a bit nervously. As she'd never had sex with him, it was an absolute impossibility. "I'm not in touch with the man who is. I just wanted to let you know what happened and tell you I understand if you don't want to go out anymore."

Hal stared at her blankly. "Do you love him—the father, I mean?"

"No," she said, frowning at the question. This wasn't at all how she had expected. What she'd expected was for him to tell her he never wanted to see her again. "I don't even know him, not really. It was one of those amazing nights, and maybe they're amazing because reality will never intrude. Or so I thought. I have a condition known as PCOS—" He nodded. "Anyway, one of the things it does is make it very difficult for a woman to get pregnant, so in a way, it's kind of a miracle."

Hal leaned across, placing his hand over Kessily's. "If you're happy, then I'm happy for you. I don't know that I'm ready to be a father…"

"Oh God, no, I wasn't asking that. I just wanted you to know and that I'd understand if you didn't want to see me again."

He smiled. He had a pleasant face and was a nice guy, but nothing about him moved her as Falkor had done.

"I also don't know that I'm not ready to be a father. Why don't we just take it one step at a time and see where it leads us. If nothing else, we can probably get to be good friends."

Why would he think she wanted him to be involved in her child's life, much less as a stand-in father. But, still, he was trying to be supportive. "I think I'd like that."

They finished their coffee and pastries and then both headed back to work. Over and over, Kessily told herself that Hal was a nice guy, and he was. It was just that 'but' that came afterward in her mind every time she reminded herself of that.

But he was dull, bordering on boring.

But I'm not attracted to him. I might have seen him as attractive enough in the past, but that night with Falkor had left her desirous of him and no one else.

But he had some annoying habits, none of which I can really articulate at the moment, but I know I always leave his company feeling somewhat annoyed and frustrated.

She made a vow to herself that she would be honest with Hal no matter what, but she knew there was no way she would make a life with him. Falkor had shown her a kind of power and passion she'd only read about in books and fantasized about at night when she slept, and there was no going back from that. She'd have it all, or she'd have nothing.

Kessily had replayed that night in her head over and over again. And somewhere along the line, she figured out she'd lost her heart to the mysterious man known only as Falkor.

CHAPTER 8

FALKOR

He could detect her scent long before the vision in his mind's eye cleared so that he could see her. Growling low in his throat, he saw her body tremble—not in fear but in anticipation and desire. She was naked, as was he, and her wrists were bound to the bed.

"Falkor, this isn't what I was anticipating," she said breathlessly.

"Nor was I, but any dream in which you are naked and aroused is one in which I will indulge."

He crawled up onto the bed, pushing her knees apart and running his finger up along her inner thigh, smiling as her body squirmed both from his scrutiny and his touch. He allowed his finger to travel up her body, completely ignoring her swollen labia and clit to trace designs all over her breasts.

Her nipples grew taut, and Falkor leaned down to suck one of them into his mouth, swirling his tongue around it before suckling, giving it a nip, and then moving to the other one. *Her hands grasped the leather bindings as her hips undulated.*

Falkor slipped his hand between her thighs, drawing a line between her throbbing nub and her warm, wet heat. He trailed his finger lightly through her labia before slipping it inside her, stroking the ceiling of her core and making her catch her breath.

"You will give me everything," he said, hovering over her. The only thing that connected them was his finger moving in and out until his hand plunged deep and he brought his thumb down on her clit.

"Falkor, please," she moaned as he slipped another finger inside her, scissoring them.

"All in good time," he breathed, allowing his heated breath to reach her quivering body.

He traveled down her body, never removing his teasing fingers and yet refraining from giving her what she needed to climax. Removing his thumb, Falkor swirled his tongue around her needy clit, giving it a gentle nip before soothing and sucking it into his mouth and flicking it with his tongue.

Kessily moaned and writhed. Just as he was about to send her over the edge, Falkor settled himself between her legs, plunging into her hard and deep. She called out his name as she wrapped her legs around him.

Falkor began pounding into her with the ferocity of a man long denied who was being given his ultimate reward. She was hot, tight, and her fever nearly matched his own. Kessily bucked up beneath him, until he slipped his hands beneath her ass, holding her in place and forcing her to take his punishing thrusts.

He could feel the rising tide and overwhelming need of her body to be one with his and he began thrusting into her at a fast and furious pace. Her inner walls shook and spasmed up and down his hard length as he increased the pleasure he was inflicting upon her.

Kessily's breath sped up and became shallower and more thready. The noises she made became more whimper than sigh as her orgasm began to wash over her. Her body stiffened and as he gave a final hard, ferocious thrust deep inside her, she screamed in ecstasy. Her pussy clamped down hard, and she writhed within his hold as she greedily milked his cock.

As she did so, Falkor groaned as his seed began to spew forth into her core and he savored every bit of pleasure as he held her in his arms.

"Let me go," she said.

"Never."

The dream slipped away like the mists at dawn—softly, quietly, and completely. Oh, the memory of the dream was there, but the luxury of living in it, of being one with her, was gone.

Falkor rolled to the side of the bed, sat up, and placed his feet on the floor. He missed her, which was silly, as he'd only been with her the one time. He'd learned long ago not to hold onto anyone too tightly as his immortality made him continue while those around him succumbed to their mortal cycle of life. Only his sister had been restored to him, but in this guise, too, her time was finite.

Kessily.

Even thinking of her brought a smile to his face. He believed her to be his eternal flame, but she was human. Did he have a right to bring her into his world? To ask her to leave her humanity behind? Could he turn his back on what he'd waited on for so long?

He really didn't question her being his eternal flame. He had known instinctively before he left her that morning. The fact that he had visceral dreams in which they were together only gave further proof that she was.

But the consequences of claiming her as such were tremendous. He would have to leave the Phantom Fire, and his immortality would be taken from him. Losing his immortality wasn't necessarily the worst thing. There were times when the unending burden seemed almost too much to carry.

Leaving the service of the Phantom Fire was another thing completely. He had been there from the first and was the only remaining warrior from the original twelve. Memory had dimmed as the millennia had stretched on. It was hard to remember the faces of those with whom he had served and even harder to remember the dragon he had once been. He had long ago forgotten what it was to be dragon only—not to have the ability to shift into a human.

And then there was the price to be paid to the Phantom Fire for his leaving—his firstborn son when he reached a certain age. He wasn't sure he could do that—wasn't sure he could condemn his son to the life he had led. And how would Kessily react? Falkor smiled at his musing; not well, he thought. How did one go about asking a drakaina to give up her child? Most drakaina were protective in the extreme of their offspring. He couldn't imagine Kessily being any different.

An image of Kessily, her belly round with his child, passed before his eyes, making his lips curve up in a smile and his cock begin to swell. That wasn't much of a surprise. Any image of Kessily that came to mind made his cock harden.

As he rose from his bed, another image came to him—Kessily as she had entered that restaurant with another man. The taste of jealousy was bitter in his mouth. She was his eternal flame—of that he had no doubt, but did he have the right to claim her as such? How did one go about claiming a drakaina that might not want to be claimed?

Things were easier in the past—a dragon simply declared a drakaina as his and took her to live with him. He chuckled, reminding himself that while that might sound easy, drakaina had a reputation for being fractious and difficult to bring to heel. The idea of such a confrontation with Kessily was proving to be interesting and arousing.

He would need to decide fairly soon if he was willing to let her slip from his grasp. The idea of the man taking Kessily to bed; hearing her moan and sigh as he pleasured her; feeling her body clench with desire and tremble beneath him as she called his name… it made him angry beyond measure.

Standing under the cold water pouring from the showerhead was doing nothing to alleviate his desire for his mate. And there it was again—his absolute certainty that she was his. Was there really any question in his mind as to what he should do? She was his eternal flame, and it was about time he started doing something about it.

Coming out of the shower, he left his dwelling and shifted from man to beast, taking to the skies as he had every morning in the time between the waning of the moon and the first rays of the new day lighting the sky. It was foolish and somewhat dangerous, but each morning he made the long trek to watch over her as she woke to ensure she was safe. Falkor snorted at his own excuse for his indulgence. He didn't believe Kessily was in any danger whatsoever. No, what he wanted to see was that she still slept alone. He wasn't absolutely convinced he wouldn't roast any man he caught leaving her bed.

That thought made him happy—not roasting the man who had taken her to dinner several times but confronting him, at the least. Perhaps that was some- thing he should do. Find out his name and then threaten him, letting him know that pursuing anything more than friendship with Kessily was not in his best interest. Yes, that was it. He was doing the man a favor. Falkor snorted again. What fools these mortals be thinking they could ever quench the fire that was his eternal flame. True, he was certain the man hadn't a clue, but Falkor intended to ensure he was apprised of all the facts. If he still pursued her, then Falkor could simply challenge him and be done with it.

He loved the blue hours between the last of the night and the beginning of the day. Not many humans were stirring, especially in the vast wilderness over which he flew. He made sure to stay above the clouds and out of the flight path of the commercial airlines, but still kept a watchful eye to ensure his presence as a dragon wasn't seen.

Falkor could feel something shifting within him—an understanding and acceptance that Kessily could and would be his. As he flew, he stretched his muscles and wings and could feel his cock beginning to throb. He smiled to himself as he soared above the clouds, tipping his wings into their airy softness, ripe with the dew that would fall to earth.

He could recall in exquisite detail the feeling of Kessily's pussy as it spasmed along his length as he thrust into her again and again, and then the exquisite sensation as he pumped his seed into her as she clamped down on him, milking him for every last bit. No woman in all of his existence had ever pleased him more, and truth be told, that was saying a lot. Falkor had had more than his fair share of women—

both drakaina and human alike. He hoped she would accept her place at his side and in his bed and be ready to be repeatedly fucked long and hard.

Falkor began to muse on how he might reinsert himself into Kessily's life. The obvious way would be to make a generous donation to the Sierra Club and become a co-plaintiff in the lawsuit against Sarkany and his company. Many years ago, the Phantom Fire had created various companies through which they could conduct business in the realm of man. One of those—Warriors of the Winds—was an environmental group and would be the perfect vehicle with which to insert himself into the lawsuit.

He almost felt sorry for Sarkany and the Firedrake Land Use Company. Almost.

CHAPTER 9

KESSILY

Falkor stood before her—naked, heavily muscled, and fully aroused. She'd never been one to judge a man's ability to pleasure her by the size of his cock, but Falkor had combined size with an innate ability to know what would make her writhe beneath him, calling his name, and clawing at his back. No wonder that one night had resulted in her becoming pregnant—god knows they'd done it enough times. Her PCOS had waved its white flag and surrendered to him.

He had her pinned to the wall before he hauled her up against his body, pinning her arms behind her back with one arm as he insinuated his thigh between hers, allowing her to feel the strength and enormity of his cock as it strained against her.

He inhaled deeply. She wondered if he really could scent her arousal. A kind of buzzing in her head was disconcerting but not frightening. Far worse was the wildfire that he seemed to ignite in her blood. Her nipples beaded in response to his nearness and her clit became engorged as a pool of liquid heat gathered at the opening of her core.

Falkor's mouth came down on hers, his lips fusing to hers as he thrust his tongue between her lips. He dominated her in a way no man had ever done before. His lips moved across hers in an expression of pure carnality and need as he crushed her sensitized breasts to his chest. He continued kissing her, nibbling along her bottom lip as he used his thigh to rub her swollen nub. Every synapse in her body came alive as the lightning of her need flashed through her system.

She moaned against his mouth, her tongue dancing with his. He repositioned her so that each time he moved his thigh, he could press and rub against her clit. Even though in some dim recess of her mind she knew this was another dream, she felt as though she should do something to make him stop—something to allow her to regain some semblance of control. But she didn't.

Instead, she tore her arms free of his grip only to grasp his bulging biceps and rock herself along his thigh—forward and back, increasing her arousal and the pleasure that surged through her system. But she wanted more. She wanted to feel him again as he pulled her beneath him, settling himself between her thighs and mounting her in a possessive and primal manner. She rolled her hips faster and faster, applying more friction to the nub between her legs as Falkor continued to kiss her, overwhelming her senses in a way she'd never even imagined possible.

"That's my good girl," he crooned. "Take your pleasure from me, for only I will give it to you in the future. You are mine, and your destiny lies with me."

Before Falkor, Kessily had never imagined such pleasure

was possible. Now she knew different and had experienced it repeatedly during a hedonistic night that had resulted in her becoming pregnant.

The fire in her blood surged through her system until only one thing existed… Falkor. There was a deep rumbling coming from him as he held her and let her ride his thigh, encouraging her with the nuzzling of her neck. She felt the desire that had been pooling in her sheath begin to leak down the inside of her thighs, soaking onto his. She should have been mortified; she wasn't. Nothing that felt this good could be wrong. Her nipples felt as if they would burst if she didn't feel his mouth upon them.

As if he could hear her thoughts, his mouth left hers and moved down her throat as his hand came up to palm her breasts. Her nipples tightened and the areolae surrounding them became puffy and overly sensitized. Falkor swirled his tongue around the area, spiraling it down before sucking the pert tip into his mouth and drawing on it deeply. She groaned in intense pleasure as she arched her body, pushing the nipple deeper into his mouth.

As he continued to suckle one nipple, he brought his hand to her other turgid peak. Pressure began to build, as did her need to experience, yet again, the ultimate rapture with this man. His hand snaked down between them until he reached her clit. She was so over-stimulated that she called his name and all but climaxed the instant he made contact.

"So much better when I play with your body than when you do it yourself," he chuckled.

His fingers slid past her nub, parting her labia until they teased the entrance to her core. Slipping his fingers just inside to tickle her inner walls, his thumb found her and pressed down hard. Kessily felt her legs tremble as pleasure swept over and she fell over the edge into a free-fall of ecstasy. She cried out as her pussy pulsed hard, clamping down on the only thing that was offered. She trembled as she writhed in his hold, savoring every bit of pleasure she could as she fell forward against him.

Kessily woke from another dream of Falkor, feeling shaken and confused. Every night it seemed she dreamt of him. If she managed to wake herself, she only went back to sleep to have the dream resume. She told herself that pregnancy played hell with your hormones and that many women found they had an increased libido either during different stages or all throughout. That might be great for a woman with a partner, but for one without, it sucked… and not in a good way.

Her mother maintained that her dreams about Falkor—not that she knew their erotic content—were her subconscious mind trying to tell her that she needed to find him and tell him, or at least try. It wasn't that she didn't think her mother was right about the subconscious part, but she also knew her mother well enough to know that somewhere deep down inside she hoped that Falkor would confess he'd been looking for her and would sweep her and the baby off to some amazing life. Kessily suspected her mother was already filing away plans for some fabulous wedding on the fly.

Truth be told, there was a miniscule part of her

that wished for the same thing, but Kessily was far too much of a realist to believe that would ever happen. The reality was, she'd be lucky if he even wanted to be any part of the life they'd created.

Kessily shook her head, trying to dispel such thoughts and to get it to focus on the things she needed to do today as she reached for the gingersnaps her mother left by her bed each night. She walked to her window, as she had every morning since she'd confirmed she was pregnant and looked up into the sky. She wasn't sure what it was she expected to see there, but whatever it was, it clearly wasn't there. Kessily couldn't quite shake the feeling that she was being watched—not necessarily in a creepy stalker way, but as though someone was watching over her to keep her and the child she carried safe.

She headed into the bath, and when she emerged, she was fully made-up, and her hair was in a messy bun. She pulled on what passed for a business suit at the Sierra Club—a mid-calf length skirt, a denim overshirt belted with a silver concho belt, a wool blazer of Native-American design, and her beloved cowboy boots. It might not cut it in corporate America or most law firms, but it suited her just fine.

"How are you feeling, honey?" asked her mother, who got up every morning now to prepare Kessily's breakfast and make sure she ate.

Taking the cup of ginger tea, Kessily answered, "Much as I hate to admit it, this gingersnap and ginger tea regimen you've got me on seems to be doing the trick. I haven't had any morning sickness since you talked me into it. But you didn't have to start baking the gingersnaps from scratch."

Her mother smiled and handed her a ham and cheese omelet. "Of course I did. You can't be eating things full of chemicals and preservatives. Besides, I like doing it. Did you decide on a color for the nursery?"

"The green sounds good."

From the moment Kessily had given her mother the go-ahead on the nursery, she'd been in decorator mode. It made Kessily happy to see how much her mother was enjoying herself. Selfishly, she was glad her mom was willing to take it on so Kessily didn't have to.

Having finished her breakfast, she headed into the office to meet with her boss and someone from the environmental group Warriors of the Winds to talk about the lawsuit they had just filed in Wyoming against the Firedrake Land Development Company. Firedrake wouldn't have hired Bruce Chapman if they didn't intend to fight the lawsuit. She knew Warriors of the Winds, or 'WoW,' as they were known, by reputation they were said to be staunch activists against those who would exploit the area's natural resources. There were even rumors that they were not above intimidating those on the opposing side. She would need to make it clear that the Sierra

Club could not be involved in such tactics—even though there had been times she would have liked them to be.

Kessily entered the headquarters of the Sierra Club and headed to her office.

"Hey, Kess," said her assistant, following her in.

"Hey, Wren," she answered, glancing at her watch. "I'm not late…"

"No, but the guy from WoW is already here, and he is just that—wow! Oh, my God, he's all kinds of tall, dark, and handsome. I think his suit costs more than I make in a month, and that's gross, not net."

Kessily laughed. "I don't really care how he looks. I'm just glad that WoW is willing to become a co-plaintiff in this action and pick up half the cost. I think it's going to be a long, drawn-out litigation."

As she'd started her prep work, it had become clear that Firedrake's plans would not be quashed easily. They had too many people in their pocket. She'd thought about trying to get a change of venue, but the odds weren't good and generally all that did was piss off the judge assigned to the case.

What concerned her was that she was half-way through her first trimester. At some point she'd have to tell her employers about her condition and would need to prep a replacement to finish the case. If she was lucky, WoW had someone that could sit second chair and take over when she had to take maternity leave.

She shook her head. She was still having trouble believing she was going to have to request maternity leave.

"Any messages or fires I need to put out before I go into this meeting?"

"No, we're good. Do you need anything?"

"I don't think so. I took everything I needed home with me last night."

She sat down to review her notes one more time. This meeting was important. It was important not only to the untouched grandeur of the land in question, but to those who called the region home. It was also important as it would show those who wanted to destroy areas like the Winds that there were those that would take up the sword and fight against them. If they could win here, it might make others think twice.

Kessily set her mouth in a determined line. She needed to talk to her boss about a plan if the trial went past her due date. Selfishly, she didn't want to tell him now for fear he'd pull her off the case. Strategically, she wanted to take the temperature of the local court and figure out not only if they could win, but how long and protracted the case might be.

She slipped into the woman's restroom to check her makeup one last time. She couldn't figure out why it was she was so concerned about how she looked. Vanity, perhaps? Especially now that Wren had told her the head of WoW was every bit as gorgeous as she'd heard. She also needed to present herself in a way that would make him feel comfortable with the Sierra Club taking the lead.

Checking herself in the mirror one more time, she turned to the side, running her hand over her belly. She didn't seem to be showing yet, but it was probably too early for that. Straightening her shoulders, she took a deep, cleansing breath, and made her way down to the smaller, more intimate conference room that took up one corner of their office space and had windows with commanding views on two sides.

She opened the door and both men stood up. "Ah, Kessily, you're here and right on time as usual," said her boss.

He might have droned on and on and actually introduced her to the gorgeous man who stood at his side. That man needed no introduction, though, and she could tell Wren for a fact that he looked even better naked than he did clothed.

Standing in front of her was the man who had sired her child—Falkor.

CHAPTER 10

FALKOR

He'd known she was here from the moment she'd entered the Sierra Club's headquarters, not that he could see her from the conference room, but he had felt her arrival. He'd managed to insinuate himself into this meeting as he'd known she'd be here, but he hadn't been exactly sure how they would proceed. That was odd for Falkor as he was known for his ability to strategize. But where Kessily was concerned he seemed only to be able to think to the next step, and then the one beyond.

When she entered the room, he had to touch the conference room table to keep himself grounded. In that instant he'd wanted nothing more than to shift into his dragon, seize her in his talons, and take her back to Dragonwyk to keep her with him forever. That was the primitive part of his brain's reaction.

The rest of him had a far more visceral reaction—his heart was seized with incredible longing, his stomach was doing flip flops, and his cock was swelling at an amazing speed.

As he inhaled her scent, the feral, primal part of his being rushed to the fore. It was slightly off, but not in an unpleasant way. He discreetly sniffed again—no, it was pure Kessily. He couldn't detect the slightest whiff of another man on her. In fact, as far as he could tell, she hadn't been with any man since him. She may have tried to scrub the scent of his seed away, but a trace still remained, and that made his lips curve up in a smile.

"Clancy, there's no need to introduce me to Kessily. We met at the gala event in Boulder."

"It's good to see you again, Falkor." Her voice was high and thin, but she covered her nerves well.

"Well, since we all seem to know each other, let's get down to business…"

They spent the next two hours going over every nuance of the proposed litigation. Falkor only heard bits and pieces. He was almost totally engrossed in his fantasies of Kessily. Fantasies he was beginning to believe were somehow destined to become reality. It didn't take more than a few minutes for his entire being to accept that he would not allow her to escape. He meant to claim her as his.

Oh, he'd tried to do the noble thing, the honorable thing, the right thing and walk away, leaving her in peace and him in command of the Phantom Fire. But hadn't he fulfilled any obligation he had to his brothers long ago? Even after he met Kessily, he was among those called on to defeat the Cherufe, and hadn't he done so? If any warrior of the Phantom Fire deserved to find his eternal flame, it was him. If others didn't agree, they could take up a sword against him, and they would fail. The woman standing in front of him was his destiny, and he meant to have her.

He'd been called north to Denali to the last battle with the Cherufe shortly after his liaison with Kessily. He hadn't questioned it; he'd just gone to battle as he'd always done for millennia. Upon his return, he'd wanted to go after her, hunt her down, and take her to mate, but what did he really have to offer her?

Granted, he had his share of the brotherhood's gold, but somehow he didn't think she'd be willing to give up their firstborn son to fulfill his obligation to the Phantom Fire. It had taken every ounce of his will to resist her siren's song and leave her alone—well, minus the stalking. It wasn't really stalking; it was more about ensuring she was safe and cared for.

It was a good thing he couldn't smell the man she'd been dating on her. Otherwise, he was pretty sure the first thing he'd do when he had her secure in Dragonwyk was come back to Denver and kill him. The thought that any man had been intimate with her after their encounter enraged him.

Fate had brought them together in Boulder; surely fate had intervened again to reunite them.

"So, as you can see, the Sierra Club is well-positioned and well-prepared to enter into litigation with Firedrake," Kessily said, seeming to conclude her presentation.

"Do you think there's any chance Firedrake will settle?" asked Clancy.

"Not a chance," answered Falkor. "I know Sarkany. He's a bastard of the first order and would love nothing better than to rape the Winds. If I thought all it would take is money, I'd have bought him off."

"I agree with Falkor. Mr. Sarkany seems quite singularly obsessed with his idea for a resort and casino." She turned to him. "Tell me Falkor, does WoW have a legal division? A lot of us involved in environmental issues know of your organization, but we don't know a lot about it."

"We're a small, privately-held and funded organization. I am a lawyer by training but have no formal education or degree. We are, however, prepared to back the Sierra Club in this fight and will happily pick up the tab for any out-of-pocket expenses and," he said, turning to Clancy, "could even be inclined to pick up a portion of Kessily's salary."

"The latter won't be necessary," stammered Clancy, "but picking up the out-of-pockets would be an extraordinary contribution and greatly appreciated."

"Consider it done. I expect Kessily to keep in close contact with me once she is settled up in Wyoming. I will be in the area, so coordinating our schedules shouldn't be all that difficult."

Falkor knew he was doing an end-run around what she might want, but at the end of the day, it was far more generous, not to mention far more subtle than his previous plan to release his dragon and simply abscond with her.

Clancy's cell phone vibrated. "Ah, it's the missus. I'll leave the two of you to coordinate. Kessily, let me know what you two decide."

The door closed behind Clancy, and they sat looking across at each other.

"I never expected to see you again," said Kessily quietly.

"Does it bother you that I'm here?"

"A little. I feel a tiny bit ambushed."

"How so?" he asked, conversationally, thinking 'ambushed' would have been in her office, with the blinds drawn, having her bent over her desk while he plowed her from behind. Falkor thought he was being exceptionally civilized.

"Obviously, you knew I worked for the Sierra Club and probably figured I would be here and probably knew I was directly involved in this litigation. I, on the other hand, had no idea that you were part of WoW and that you planned to be here today."

"What would that have changed?"

"What do you mean?"

Falkor cocked his head. "Would you not have come into the office had you known I would be here? Or perhaps not agreed to head up the legal team in Wyoming?"

"We agreed never to see each other again."

"No. I told you there was someplace I had to be. I had previous obligations. I have now attended to those and am back."

"Did WoW get involved because of me?" she asked.

"Only partially. I want to see Sarkany stopped for all kinds of reasons, but I have other means of dealing with him. When I heard the Sierra Club was filing suit and that you would be lead counsel, I saw it as an ideal way to re-enter your life."

"You were never in my life…"

"Only because of the previous commitments I had. Does my being here upset you?" he asked.

"No. Not really."

Falkor stood and took her by the hand. "Then let's get out of here and go someplace we can talk."

"I don't think that's a good idea. In fact, I think I should recuse myself. I'll let Clancy know. We have several litigators on staff who could do a good, if not better, job than I."

"Unacceptable."

"What? You can't just decide unilaterally that things are going to go your way."

Falkor chuckled. How little she knew. "I think you'll find I can do just that."

He tried to lead her out of the doorway, but she balked and pulled back.

"This is not a good idea," she said, trying, he thought, to remain civil and professional.

While civil and professional Kessily was impressive, it was wild, uninhibited Kessily he wanted to get back inside of.

Releasing her hand only to grasp her by the upper arm, he pulled her close. "Either you walk out of here under your own steam, or I swear I'll toss you over my shoulder and carry you out."

They stood facing each other. When she did nothing other than stare at him, he tightened his grip and began to walk/drag her toward the elevator. He marveled that while all of the little heads popped up out of their cubicles to gape at him as he strode toward the elevator with Kessily in tow, not one person said so much as a word. A buzz of whispers trailed after him as he moved them into the bank of elevators, punching the down button.

Dragging Kessily into the first elevator that arrived, he shoved her against the mirror-and-walnut-paneled wall and once the elevator had started down, pressed the emergency stop button, answering the phone as it rang.

"Who is this?" Falkor growled.

"I'm Arturo. I'm with maintenance."

"Arturo, I have one thousand dollars if you'll turn off this alarm and tell people it's out of service for the next thirty to forty minutes."

"Yes, sir. I can make that happen," said Arturo.

"Good man."

Kessily rolled her eyes. "Seriously? What do you think you're going to do in here?"

"This," he rumbled, as his mouth came down on hers.

One fist came up to tangle in her hair and give it a light tug. Kessily moaned and not in a you-hurt-me kind of way, but more in a tone that let him know she'd missed him as well. His other hand wrapped around her waist and drifted down to cup her buttocks. His hips moved as if of their own accord so that he was pressed hard against her. Hard being the operative word.

Kessily moved against him, rubbing herself until he stepped back. She stepped with him, trying not to allow any break in contact. It seemed to him that she liked the feel of his hard cock against her belly. Leaning in, she parted her lips, offering her mouth to him.

Tilting her head back, his tongue thrust past her teeth, tangling with hers. His fist in her hair allowed him to angle her head just the way he wanted as he plundered her mouth. The feral lust that she had unleashed in him seemed to wash over them both and release a similar feeling in her. Her body melted into his, and she kissed him back with the inflamed passion he remembered from Boulder.

Falkor unbuckled her belt and ran his hands up under her shirt, pushing her bra up so he could get at her naked breasts. He palmed and cupped them, running his hands over them and plucking at her nipples with his fingers.

"Falkor, no…"

"Kessily, yes," he chuckled as he gave her hair another tug, exposing her throat to him.

He kissed his way from her mouth down her throat, nibbling as he went and rucking up her skirt with his free hand. She only pushed at his hand once, and when he nipped her ear she ceased struggling. Finding a pair of skimpy panties between him and the prize he sought, he ripped them away from her body, bringing them to his nostrils to inhale her scent. Again, he was caught off guard by something being off—not wrong, but different.

"Hey, I don't have many of those. They're expensive," she complained.

Falkor stuffed them in his pocket. "You won't be needing them anymore. You are never to wear panties again."

He unbuttoned his fly, releasing his throbbing

dick. Pressing her against the wall, he released his hold on her hair and lifted her off the floor, holding her poised above his cock. His eyes locked with hers as he lowered her onto him, impaling her completely. Her legs wrapped around his waist, and her arms came around him.

Falkor kissed her again as he began to fuck up inside her. He had lived thousands of years, and nothing had ever compared to the exquisite pleasure of Kessily's pussy hugging his cock. He grasped her ass and slid her up and down the wall as he moved her, making the connection deeper and more complete.

Over and over, he thrust up into her, only to retreat and thrust again. He could feel her body stiffening in anticipation, and he drove into her again and again, until she arched her back, called his name and her pussy clamped down as he sent her careening over the edge. He thrust into her a final time, his body shuddering as he came, sending his seed into her to find her womb and take root.

He knew, even as he finished, that she was what he had waited for. She was the prize he had earned for his service. She would grow ripe with his son, and he would ensure that unless he felt called to the brotherhood, no one would take the product of their union from them.

CHAPTER 11

KESSILY

Fuck! Fuck! Fuck! What had she done? Was she nuts? It was this kind of madness that had gotten her into this mess in the first place. If she'd only kept her head in Boulder, she wouldn't now be carrying his child and wouldn't have just fucked him in a public elevator.

"Mine," he growled low as he nuzzled her throat before lifting her off his cock, pushing her skirt back down and stuffing his cock back into his jeans.

Kessily straightened her skirt and stooped down to pick up her belt, which meant she was eye level with his cock, which seemed to be determined to become engorged again and escape the fly he was buttoning up. Standing up quickly, she wrapped the belt around her waist and buckled it.

She turned her back to look in the mirror. Kessily tried to search her purse for a tissue or something with which to wipe away the smeared lipstick. Before she could do so, his hand was in front of her offering a handkerchief. There was something definitely *old world* about Falkor. Something that seemed out of place with their times, but integral to his being.

Taking the handkerchief she said, "Thank you. I guess I can cross that one off my list. Now all I need is to join the Mile High Club."

A funny grin crossed his face as he dropped a kiss to her shoulder. "I think I can help you with that, in more ways than one."

Now what the hell did he mean by that?

She looked at her hair. It was a complete disaster. No way was she going to get it put back up on her head. In the mirror's reflection, she saw him reach back to release the emergency stop button.

She turned in his arms. "I don't think I'm going to be pulled back together before we hit the lobby. Anyone looking will know what we did," she said trying to reach past him.

He stayed her hand. "I don't care. They'll all know soon enough."

"Maybe you don't, but what if I do?"

"You don't." He leaned in close, resting his forehead against hers. "You and I both know that what just happened was more than just a nice fuck. I think we've both always known Boulder wasn't a one and done, and that we were meant to be together. I've tried telling myself over and over that there are a lot of reasons we will never work, even more that we shouldn't even try, but none of them seem to override the most logical conclusion."

He could think logically? She could barely think at all, much less logically. "And what's that?"

He kissed her tenderly, almost reverently, "That we belong together."

Kessily shoved at his chest, making him step back. "Don't say that! How can you say that? We know next to nothing about each other, and we've had sex. I'll grant you it's spectacular sex, but it's just sex."

He closed on her so that she was surrounded by him. Instead of saying the wrong thing—or even the right thing—he settled his mouth on hers and kissed her tenderly but with a growing passion. God he was a good kisser. She didn't normally enjoy kissing, but she could well imagine spending hours kissing Falkor.

Tell him, whispered the little voice inside her head. She couldn't; she wouldn't. Right now, this baby belonged to her. If she told him, she'd have to share it. She knew as well as she knew her own name. The man holding her close and drugging her with kisses was not a man to walk away from his child or what he perceived to be his obligation.

The opening of the elevator door broke her reverie, and she snapped back into reality. *What the hell did I just do?*

Ending the kiss, she stepped away and headed into the lobby. He followed her out, and she shook his hand. "It's been nice to see you again. I have an appointment I need to get to."

"You're not going to walk away from me, Kessily," he said in a voice that told her he was annoyed and was used to having his wishes obeyed.

"Sure, I am," she said brightly. "Just watch."

Going to the curb, she hailed a cab. As the cab driver slowed, Kessily reached out to open the door. Just as quickly, Falkor dismissed the driver and shut the door firmly.

"I'm not done with you yet."

"That's too bad, because I am done with you, at least for the time being." *Why the hell did I add that last part? I am done with him. I have to be. I can't function properly. One touch of his hand and my mind goes into neutral, and my libido goes into overdrive.* "Like it or not, I have someplace else I need to be. Now, please leave me alone."

The 'someplace' she needed to be was with her mother. Kessily felt an almost overwhelming need to speak with her. As close as they had always been, they were even closer now. She needed her mother's calm, supportive voice to help her think through what she was feeling. She needed to let her know she'd seen Falkor again and was in desperate need of her advice. Kessily didn't think she'd share with her that she had another round of mind-bending sex with him. Some things her mother really didn't need to know, although she suspected there was very little that got past her.

He muttered something that sounded like 'easier

when you just dragged them off to your cave…' but Kessily couldn't quite be sure.

"You can't just dismiss my cab that way," she said in a far sharper tone than she had intended.

"I think you'll find I do pretty much as I like." He lifted up his hand and a sleek Cadillac Escalade pulled up. Falkor opened the door. "Get in."

"No. Now go away."

"I'm not going anywhere without you. Please get in."

"No. I don't want to go with you. I told you I have places to go and people to see."

"Then my driver and I will take you wherever you need to go and wait for you until you are free."

"Do you understand the meaning of the word no? I'm not going anywhere with you. Leave me alone."

Kessily spun on her heel, intending to leave him standing on the sidewalk, staring after her. Once more, Falkor grabbed her upper arm, using her inertia to spin her back around and direct her into the SUV. She all but fell onto the back seat. As Falkor climbed in, she reached for the door handle on the other side of the vehicle.

"Enough," he growled, impeding her progress and pulling her away from the door. The SUV pulled away from the curb. "Now, where are we going?"

Kessily sat silently, trying to run the scenarios available to her. Nothing came. Absolutely nothing. He was too big and too strong to try and overpower.

She doubted the windows were unlocked, but she tried them surreptitiously anyway to no avail. That meant no rolling down the window and screaming for help.

Of course, she could always tell him she was pregnant and wait for him to put her out on the nearest street corner, but she didn't think there was a snowball's chance in hell that he would do that. *Why is it I am so reluctant to tell him? And how do I know that it is an irrevocable choice to make? Once he knows, there will be no excluding him from my life and that of our child.*

"Would you like to go to my hotel?" he asked, politely.

Would I like to? Hell, yeah. I'd like to get naked with you and go another couple of rounds. What she said instead was, "I'd like you to take me back to my office. My meetings with clients are confidential. In fact, my clients are confidential."

She had him there.

Kessily continued, "And everything I do for that client is also confidential."

"Perhaps, but do you really expect me to believe that you had anywhere at all to go?"

"Are you calling me a liar?" she accused.

"No. I just don't believe you were going anywhere that had anything to do with your work."

"Well, my private life is none of your concern."

"What if I want to make it my concern?"

Kessily hadn't expected that. In fact, she hadn't

expected any of this. She hadn't planned to have a one-night stand in Boulder. She hadn't planned to, against all odds, get pregnant. She hadn't ever expected to see the father of that baby again. She sure as hell hadn't planned to have sex in an elevator with him. And she hadn't planned to be riding around in a luxury SUV with him being interrogated.

Okay, that last part wasn't true—well the riding around in a luxury SUV was, but he wasn't doing anything, which on the face of it wasn't a nice thing to do. Her problem, and she damn well knew it, was that she was hiding something from him. Something which he had a right to know. Her mother had been every kind of supportive about the pregnancy. The one sticking point between them was that her mother believed Falkor had a right to know he had fathered a child.

If she truly believed he'd want nothing to do with it, it would be simple enough to just inform him, have him sign relinquishment papers, and move on with her life. But what had at first been a kind of unrealistic dream of finding some kind of happily ever after with the enigmatic man sitting beside her had become a kind of soul crushing reality. She believed Falkor would want to be a part of his child's life, but not the life of the woman who had borne him or her. And that, she realized as she sat beside him, breathing in his clean, masculine scent, was the crux of her problem.

"Kessily is there something bothering you? You seemed flustered at the meeting."

She gave a little laugh. "Well, I wasn't exactly expecting to see the man I spent fucking his brains out in a hotel in Boulder sitting beside my boss. You know, that was a pretty shitty thing to do—not the banging my brains out, but the sitting beside my boss. You might have given me a heads up, but you didn't. Why is that?"

"Because I wanted to see you again, and I was afraid you might avoid the meeting."

"You wanted to see me again?"

He nodded. "When I walked away from you in Boulder, I told myself it was the right thing to do. I told myself it was for the best, and I was doing the noble thing. What I've realized over the past couple of months is that I don't want to be noble about you. I want to be greedy and selfish. But mostly, I want you."

CHAPTER 12

KESSILY

*N*othing he might have said could have shocked her more. He could have told her he was an alien from outer space, and it would have had less of an impact. Not knowing what else to do and having absolutely nothing to say, she punched him in the arm.

"You do not get to say that to me."

"That hurt, you know," he said rather blandly. "And why shouldn't I tell you what I know to be true?"

"You do not know that."

"I do, as evidenced by our coupling in the elevator. I assure you that is not something I normally do. In fact, as with you, it was the first time I have ever done so."

"Really?" she asked.

"Really," he answered with a ghost of a smile playing around the corners of his mouth.

That, too, shocked her. She could easily imagine Falkor having sex in all kinds of places with all kinds of beautiful women—far more beautiful than she was. It wasn't that she had a bad self-image; Kessily just prided herself on being a realist. Falkor was gorgeous —tall, muscular, and he had such a magnetic and mesmerizing presence. And if this SUV was any indication, he had money and lots of it. He was the kind of man who should have supermodels hanging off him, and yet here he sat, telling her he wanted her.

Not knowing what else to say, she asked simply, "Why?"

"Because you are beautiful, intelligent, intriguing, and you move me in a way no other woman ever has."

Kessily shook her head. "You just put it right out there, don't you?"

"We are both adults. I see no reason not to be straightforward and honest about my intentions and feelings."

Did he have to be so nice and reasonable about everything?

"Would you like to tell me where you were going? I do think we need to sit down and talk, but if you're too busy at the moment, you can let me know what will work for you."

"Could you please stop being so reasonable? We both know you were right. I just wanted to get out of the building to get away from you. So now you know. Could you get the driver to just pull over and drop me off?"

"I am not just going to strand you in the middle of Denver."

"I won't be stranded; I'll hail a cab."

"Which seems like a complete waste of your time and money. Tell me where you'd like to go, and I'll be happy to drop you there."

"Fine. Take me back to the Sierra Club. I have work to do."

"Then what?"

"What do you mean then what? Then I'll go home and have dinner with my mother before working on whatever I brought home because I didn't get it done because I was too busy fucking you in an elevator and driving idly around Denver."

He chuckled. "Then if it's my fault you have to take work home, how about if I buy you dinner?"

"No. I promised my mother I'd pick up a couple of good steaks and some artisanal bread for dinner tonight."

"Good. I'd like to meet your mother. I know an excellent butcher. Why don't I select the steaks and pick you up at, say, six? That way you won't have to take work home."

"I have my own vehicle…"

"Fine. I'll meet you in the Sierra Club lobby and you can drive me to your place. I can arrange to be picked up at the end of what I'm sure will be an enjoyable and enlightening evening."

Kessily wasn't quite sure how he'd managed it, but he had managed to neatly box her in, which she was sure had been his intent.

"Better make it six thirty. You've wasted a lot of my time this morning."

Falkor leaned in, running his hand up her thigh. "We both know it wasn't a waste. While you're sitting at your desk with no panties on, I want you to think about how it felt to be impaled on my cock as I fucked your sweet pussy and emptied my seed into you."

Oh, fuck. It was already going to be hard enough to focus on work; now, it would be next to impossible.

"And here I was thinking you were a nice, polite man."

"No, you weren't. You know better than that. You were thinking about how much you liked it, how it made you feel alive, and how much you wanted to do it again."

"You're an arrogant bastard; I'll give you that."

Falkor chuckled and settled back as they pulled in along the curb. "I've been accused of worse," he said as the SUV came to a stop and he opened the door, stepping out and extending his hand to her.

Against her better judgment, she took it and had planned to simply walk away. The truth of the matter was that she planned to walk inside the building, wait until he left, and then run like a scared child down to the parking lot where she would jump in her vehicle and make a beeline for the safety of home and her mother.

Before she could move away from him, he tightened his grip on her arm. "And you will think of it, won't you?"

It was more command than question. It was also unnecessary. She had been pretty sure that she would be reliving the memory of the way he'd so effortlessly lifted her up before settling her on his cock and the way she'd felt as he thrust up into her before she called his name and he emptied himself into her for a good long while.

At six-thirty she left her office, and as promised, Falkor was waiting for her. He escorted her into the elevator with an old world, gentlemanly charm that disappeared the second the doors closed. Falkor moved her back against the wall, slipping his hand beneath her hair to grasp the back of her neck as the other one pulled up her skirt to caress the inside of her thigh. She could feel his breath on her lips.

"I have missed you," he said as his mouth closed over hers and he kissed her, his tongue tangling with hers as she pressed herself against him.

She'd missed him, too. At first the kiss was sweet and not at all dominating, but when her lips parted, that all changed. Gone was the teasing, coaxing kiss, and in its place was the overpowering, intoxicating tenor she had come to expect. His tongue surged in, sliding over and around her own and encouraging it to dance with his.

His fist tightened in her hair, emphasizing both the control he had as well as the way he seemed able to possess her with just a kiss—although that was a bit of a misnomer. There was nothing 'just' about it.

The elevator came to a stop, and he broke it off. When she opened her eyes, Kessily thought she'd see triumph or a smirk, but there was none of that. All she saw was a deep contentment that seemed to echo the purr she could feel coming from him. There was no sound, just a resonant humming that seemed to have taken up residence within her.

"Did you get the steaks? Did I tell you we needed three?"

He held up a bag from the most expensive butcher in Denver. "I did, indeed. I also picked up two loaves of bread—one is a lovely garlic and cheese focaccia, and the other is a good artisanal French bread with a crispy crust and the soft, fluffy interior that kind of bread is known for. I also took the liberty to pick up some French cream butter."

Kessily laughed. "What the hell is the difference between French cream butter and regular butter? I should warn you that if my mother knows it's French anything, she'll adore you. She spent a summer in Paris as a young woman. She loves anything French."

"She's never been back? Have you ever been?"

"No and no. After my father left us, money

was tight—really tight. It wasn't until I was halfway through law school that I realized just how tight. So, I didn't have any luxuries as a child, but I had all I needed, and I had my mother's love."

Even though she was driving, he helped her into her SUV, heading around to the passenger side and putting the bags on the back seat.

"If your mother loves anything French, we should stop and get a nice French Cab…"

"My mother doesn't care for Cabernet Sauvignon."

"How about Malbec?"

"Isn't that Argentinian?"

"Many people incorrectly assume that, as seventy-five percent of it is now produced there, but actually its origins and creation are in France."

"You just made my mother's day. She loves Malbec, and once she knows it's French, it will be her wine of choice."

They rode the rest of the way with Falkor asking all the things one does when getting to know someone. As she exited the highway, he asked, "What made you decide to become a lawyer?"

"I love hiking and camping. I used to have a favorite place to go on the Front Range. It got bought and developed into a resort. It's a beautiful resort, but that wilderness is gone forever. I was one of many who signed petitions in opposition, but there was no one to take them to court and stop them. I wanted to change that."

"Understandable. I, too, love to be out in the mountains and see them as they were hundreds of years ago—unspoiled and unsullied. There's nothing quite like it."

"I don't know. Sex with you, if it isn't better, is a close second."

Did I just say that?

"I would have to agree with that."

They stopped at an exclusive wine shop and Falkor emerged with two bottles of wine. When they arrived at her house, he helped her out of the vehicle, picked up the packages, and escorted her inside.

"Mom? I'm home. I brought a friend for dinner," she called.

"From bastard to friend in less than a day," he whispered in her ear.

"I hope they like potatoes lyonnaise and haricots verts," replied her mother.

"He thinks those are the perfect accompaniment to the gorgeous New York steaks, artisanal bread, French butter, and Malbec we picked up on the way home," called Falkor.

As Kessily knew it would, that made her mother pop her head out from the kitchen. "Malbec and French butter? Oh, Kessily, I like him already."

Kessily rolled her eyes. "Falkor, this is my mother Maribelle…"

"Everyone calls me Meri," said her mother, extending her hand.

Taking her mother's hand, he brought it to his lips and placed a chaste kiss on it. "I am Falkor. Your daughter has told me such lovely things about you."

Her mother shot her a look before bestowing a dazzling smile on Falkor. "She hasn't said a thing about you—the naughty girl."

Falkor chuckled. "She can be, but then she is so wonderful in every other way, it is hard not to forgive any small shortcomings she has."

"Falkor and I met in Boulder."

Her mother's head whipped back around to examine Falkor more closely. "Boulder?"

"Yes," he replied. "I was at the gala in which your daughter was honored."

"I knew Kessily met someone, but bad girl that she is, she never mentioned that someone was such a gorgeous hunk. Are you a male model?"

"Alas, no. Merely a businessman who believes in the same environmental causes as Kessily."

Her mother nodded. "We have always been pro-environment in this house."

"Do you have an outdoor grill?" asked Falkor. "If you like I can have these steaks ready in no time. I had the butcher use his special rub as I thought it would give it time to sink in. Now all I need to know is how do you like your steak?"

"I'm perfectly capable of grilling the steaks,"

asserted Kessily, feeling a bit peevish but wondering why.

"What Kessily meant to say is that we both prefer our steaks medium rare."

"Excellent. Kessily, I believe you are capable of doing anything you want. But if I grill the steaks while you help Meri with the rest of the meal and getting the table ready, it'll be done twice as fast. And before you ask, if you give me meat and some kind of fire, I can keep you fed. That is the sum total of my culinary expertise. I am, however, quite adept at clean up."

"The grill is right outside. You'll find both propane and charcoal, but the charcoal may be too damp to get it to light properly."

Falkor grinned and removed the steaks from their bag, holding them in the butcher paper in which they were wrapped. "I'm quite adept with fire, as well."

He headed outside. The door was barely closed before her mother rounded on her.

"That's him?"

"Yes. Don't make anything of his being here. He's become a co-plaintiff in the case up in Wyoming…"

"Well, isn't that nice," her mother said with her smile growing wider by the minute.

"Mother, don't make a big thing, okay?"

"Why shouldn't I? The man who is the father of my grandchild is gorgeous, charming and apparently more interested in you than you are in him."

"I didn't say I wasn't interested, but honestly,

mother, you saw him. He's gorgeous. And from what I can tell he's very wealthy."

"You say that like those are bad things."

"They're not, but I don't want him to be involved with the baby because he feels obligated."

"Not to put too fine a point on it, darling, but he is obligated. He made that baby just as much as you did."

She was able to shut her mother up and get the rest of dinner ready and the table set before Falkor came in with what appeared and smelled to be perfectly grilled steaks. And unless she missed her guess, he'd been able to use the charcoal grill.

"Those smell divine, Falkor. We set up dinner in the little dining room right out here," said her mother, escorting their guest, who held both her and her mother's chairs until they were seated.

The dinner conversation was interesting, but they avoided controversial topics such as religion and politics. She and her mother helped Falkor clear the table and begin cleaning up. He quickly refilled her mother's glass with Malbec, but she once again politely refused.

As Falkor was finishing up, Kessily excused herself and walked out into the small garden. It was damp. She wondered how he'd managed to light the charcoals. She breathed in the night air and was surprised when she felt his presence as he spun her around, pressed her back against a tree and lowered his head to kiss her. Who needed French Malbec wine? Falkor's kisses were all she needed to feel drunk.

"I've been wanting to do that all night," he murmured against her lips. Kessily struggled, but when he tightened his hold, she gave up. "What is it? You've been on edge ever since you introduced me to your mother, who, by the way, is charming. Are you afraid she knows what happened in Boulder or in the elevator?"

"It's not that. To be honest, she seems to like you a great deal, and I appreciate how charming you've been to her. But it would take a whole lot more than a one-night stand or a tryst in an elevator to shock my mother. In fact, she'd probably be proud of me. She tends to think I'm something of a stick in the mud."

"Then what is it? I can tell you're hiding something. If not from her, then it must be from me. What is it?"

"Kessily? Falkor?" called her mother, stepping out of the house onto the deck. "Are you all right?"

"We're fine, Meri. I'm trying to seduce your daughter," called Falkor, a discernible chuckle underlying his tone.

"I think that train has left the building, don't you think?"

Kessily could feel the change in him. His attention was diverted from Kessily to her mother.

"She told you about Boulder?" he asked quietly.

"Well, she didn't have much choice when she told

me she was pregnant." Everything in Falkor went still as her mother continued. "Actually, what she told me was either it was you or an immaculate conception with a god. Seeing you, I'd say it was a toss-up between the two."

"Trust me, Meri, there was nothing immaculate about this conception." His gaze was flinty. "Was there Kessily?"

She had meant to tell him. She was going to tell him—just not now and not like this.

CHAPTER 13

FALKOR

She was pregnant? How could that be? Dragons were not supposed to be able to impregnate humans. It was one of the main reasons the warriors of the Phantom Fire did not have sex with drakaina. How had this happened? Well, he knew the how—but how had it happened with this human woman?

Had she been with someone before they met? Or after? It couldn't be his. How would it be to raise another man's child? How would that child fare in the realm of dragons? If it was a son, would it be accepted by the Phantom Fire? Since its inception, no member of the Phantom Fire had been turned; all had been born dragon.

Falkor looked down at her. "Is this true?" He sniffed along her neck—he knew the answer but wanted to hear it from her lips, anyway.

Drawing in a deep breath, Kessily looked up at him, her lower lip trembling. Suddenly a lot of things made sense. Her distance and nervousness, as well as her almost instantaneous response to his presence. He knew many human females experienced an increased libido in the latter part of their first trimester and during the entire second. Drakaina, however, became close to insatiable during their entire pregnancy. His dick began to stiffen as it realized it had been missing out.

"Um. Yes."

"And you thought to keep this from me?"

"Not exactly. I didn't think there was even the remotest possibility that I could get pregnant. I have a condition that the doctors told me would make pregnancy a very slim possibility, so I quit taking birth control. I wasn't expecting to meet anyone in Boulder and then you came along."

Falkor drew back but did not release his hold on her. His feelings were confusing. Part of him was in disbelief; part of him was angry that she carried a child sired by someone other than him. He was not worried about siring children on her. It would seem his eternal flame was very fertile. Transitioning from human to drakaina would correct whatever this condition was that she spoke of.

"How far along are you?"

She looked at him, confusion wrinkling her brow. "What do you mean?"

"When was the baby conceived?"

"What do you mean 'when?'"

"It is a question to which I deserve an answer," he growled.

"You deserve an… hold it, just what are you asking me?"

"Do you know the name of the father?"

"Do I… what are you thinking—that I slept around in Boulder, or perhaps I fuck every guy that comes into the office in the elevator?"

Falkor flinched. It wasn't something he did. Very little took him by surprise, and that which did very rarely was of enough importance to provoke a physical reaction.

"You bastard," she snarled as she kicked him in the shin. "Get out. Do you hear me? Get out! If you come near me again, I'll take out a fucking restraining order. You're right, I'd fucked a guy the night before and the night after. My mother's been wanting me to hook up with the son of one of her friends. I fucked him, too, but frankly he was lousy in the sack."

She was breathing hard, making her breasts heave. God, she was gorgeous. She kicked his other shin. She had a temper and a mean streak, as well. No matter, fire was fire and could be turned to ignite her libido.

"Why are you still here?" she snarled. "Get out! Mom, call the cops and tell them an officer of the court is being threatened and needs assistance."

Falkor backed off. "As you wish," he said quietly and turned to walk away. He nodded to her mother. "Meri."

He left them—anger and resentment beginning to build within him. He continued to put distance between himself and Kessily. How could she have treated him like this? Any man she had been with before he could forgive as long as she never saw him again. But to have others after what passed between them? Unfathomable.

On the other hand, it wasn't as if she belonged to him. He hadn't even claimed her, much less turned her. The sex in Boulder had been wild, primal, and meaningful, at least to him. He'd begun to think at last he had been gifted with an eternal flame, but he had turned away from her. This afternoon it felt like they had connected in a deeper way, even though the sex in the elevator had been somewhat feral. He smiled. It had also been amazing.

Had the gods punished his arrogance by gifting her with a child sired by another? Had they deemed her worthy, but not him? Nothing made sense. Clearly, she belonged to someone else, or at the very least, she was having someone else's baby. He would not stand in the way of her happiness or deny another man his child. He had to respect that, didn't he?

Falkor found a place away from the road, hidden in a copse of trees. He called forth his dragon and after checking to ensure there were no witnesses, he took to the sky, making an almost completely vertical assent to climb high above the clouds. He spread his wings and banked towards Wyoming. He would be home in the Winds before dawn kissed the sky with the sun's rays.

Falkor entered Dragonwyk long before the home of the Phantom Fire was stirring. He entered his dwelling and headed into the shower. Normally he found flying freed his mind and he was able to see the solutions to problems that had somehow escaped him previously. But this flight had not given him cool resolve and acceptance. Instead, it had churned in his gut and made him angry and resentful.

He was supposed to return to the Sierra Club next week for another meeting, but the thought of seeing Kessily and being able to control himself seemed unobtainable. He had to accept that she was his eternal flame but belonged to another. But did the two negate each other? Why did he have to give her up? After all, the father of her child hadn't done so. If she was his eternal flame, as he believed more with each passing moment, then didn't he owe it to them both to do whatever was necessary?

When he exited his bath, Sobek was standing before him. "Trouble?" Falkor asked.

"I don't know, Alpha, you tell me. You go to

Boulder to have us join a lawsuit. You practically kidnap one of the lawyers and have Nadon drive the two of you around. Then you drop her off and proceed to go to a butcher, a baker, and a creamery before dismissing him and sending him home. I take it the fair lawyer was Kessily?"

"Yes."

"Then if the course of true love runs true, why are you back here alone?"

"It might run true, but it doesn't necessarily go straight from Point A to Point B. Sometimes there's a bit of a wiggle in the path."

"I've never known you to let a small wrinkle in a plan derail you."

"And it hasn't this time. It threw me for a bit of a loop, but I have come to the conclusion that Kessily is in fact my eternal flame, and I will claim her as such, but I need your help."

"You have but to ask," intoned Sobek solemnly.

"My mate carries the child of another. I need to know who that is. There is a meeting next week and I need you to attend in my stead."

"Of course, I will do as you ask, but may I ask why?"

"Because I have yet to get a handle on my more primitive leanings. Right now, I'd like to roast the bastard alive until he is nothing more than a pile of ash. But I realize that may be a bit of an over-reaction."

"Just a bit," agreed Sobek with a grin.

"I need you to ensure my mate is protected and that all is well with her."

"And then what? I understand you mean to claim her, but what of the child. Will she give it up?"

"I would not ask her to do that. When he or she is of an age, I will offer to turn them, as well. But I will raise the child as my own."

"Your will be done," said Sobek as he left Falkor.

If only it would go that smoothly with my mate.

KESSILY

The week after she told Falkor she was pregnant, there had been a client meeting scheduled. She had wondered how she would react to seeing Falkor again, but the point had been made moot when a man named Sobek had attended instead. *Why did he and Falkor only use a single name? For that matter, was it their first or their last?*

Sobek was nice, friendly, but always very respectful and professional. No chance he was going to shove her up against the wall of the elevator and fuck her senseless. The only off-putting thing about him was that every once in a while, she caught him staring at her belly. It was almost as if he knew she was pregnant, which was impossible as the only people outside her and her doctor's office who knew were her mother and Falkor.

At first, she had resented his presence and treated him like an interloper, but as the weeks turned into a month, she found herself growing closer to him. He'd taken to inviting her to lunch or being at the same coffee shop in the mornings. She'd switched to ginger tea instead of coffee or lattes. Sobek was easy to work with, and together they'd been able to identify some long-standing precedents in the statutes pertaining to land that were going to be a big help in putting a stop to Firedrake's plans to build a casino and resort.

Bruce Chapman could kiss her ass. There was no way he was going to pull out a win for Firedrake.

Falkor. The very thought of him made her heart clench and her brain snarl. She really hadn't thought he'd be the kind of guy to run at the very idea of pregnancy. She would have bet money that he would want to be involved in his child's life, but apparently not. Once the baby was born, she would send him a document terminating his parental rights so he would know she wasn't going to try and force him into anything.

For now, Kessily threw herself into work and allowed her mother to fuss over her, her diet, the nursery, and everything else on the home front. Her mom was in all her glory and having a ball. It was nice because Kessily knew everything would be taken care of and she could focus on the upcoming trial.

She knew in her heart that her determination to win was being fired to a new pitch by wanting to compensate for Falkor's rejection—not only of her, but of their child. She'd been a fool to think a man like that would want to get tied down to a woman like her or be saddled with the responsibilities of raising a child. She should have taken the time to check him out and make sure he was who she had thought him to be before ever introducing him to her mother. His easy charm and stunning good looks, combined with the Malbec, had made her mother a little tipsy, and she'd spilled the beans long before Kessily was ready to do so.

She'd risked her heart, and she guessed it had worked out the way it was supposed to. At least it had happened early on, and her child would be spared from being raised by a father who didn't care.

Another dull date with Hal. She only acquiesced to see him again as her mother kept pushing her, and Hal seemed pretty insistent. She didn't understand why, but he was. Tonight she had agreed to let him pick her up and take her home. She wasn't sure what the significance was to him, but as it didn't matter to her, she'd agreed.

He got out of the car and helped her out. "I had a lovely time, as usual, Kessily."

"Thanks, Hal. I'm sorry I get so moody. They say it's normal with pregnancy."

"I wouldn't know, but I do know you work too hard."

"Actually, I don't."

"Have your employers given you a hard time about being an unwed mother?"

Kessily had to stifle a laugh. "Well, first, it's not that big of a deal anymore, and second, by law, there's not a damn thing they could do. Besides which, they don't know."

"I'm an extremely observant individual."

Kessily's hand went to her belly. "I'm not showing, am I?"

Hal shook his head. "Not to someone not looking for it."

"I don't want to talk about him."

"I know, but if that ever changes, I am here."

They were standing on the porch when Hal leaned in to give her a peck on her cheek. He'd never tried to kiss her, which was good as she wasn't sure she wouldn't have puked on him. Just before his lips reached their target, his car alarm went off. Reaching into his pocket, he took out his key fob, pointed it at the car, and switched it off. He grinned sheepishly before trying again. Once more the alarm on his car was triggered by nothing.

Maybe someone was trying to tell them, even a chaste kiss was not a good idea.

Hal switched it off again. "I guess I'd better go. I'll have it looked at in the morning."

"Probably best," she said. "Good night, Hal."

"Good night, Kessily. Tell your mother I said hello."

"Will do."

She watched as he got in the car and drove off. Kessily turned to put the key in the lock and thought she saw something in her peripheral vision. When she turned to focus on it, nothing was there. It wasn't the first time she'd felt as if someone was stalking her. Maybe paranoia was another one of those interesting facets of pregnancy nobody told you about.

Shrugging her shoulders, she entered the house.

CHAPTER 14

FALKOR

Kessily. Thoughts of her filled his waking hours until he managed to tamp them down and push them away, but it was impossible to banish her from his dreams. Each night it was a battle to see if he could rouse himself from the dream or was forced to endure it to its end. In the morning when he woke, he either had a raging hard-on from an incomplete dream or a puddle of semen in his bed from a completed one. In either case he took a cold shower. He was beginning to wonder if he'd ever feel hot water pelting down on him again.

He raged at the gods that they would put him through this torture. Was there some lesson to be learned? They had shown him his eternal flame, but when he'd been caught between desire and duty, they had snatched her away and allowed another to take her to mate.

Or had they? Sobek had remained in Denver to watch over her. He reported that she saw no one other than the son of her mother's friend. Sobek was certain Hal wasn't the father. First, he avoided any contact with Kessily's growing belly. It was still only a slightly rounded bump, but it was there. Second, the idiot hadn't even tried to kiss her.

Well, not properly. Falkor knew that Hal had tried to kiss her once. The one time he'd tried to kiss her on her cheek, unbeknownst to anyone, Falkor had been there and had set off Hal's car alarm twice, and Hal had ended up leaving without any kiss at all—as well it should be. If anyone was going to be kissing Kessily other than her baby's sire, it would be him. He felt he had done poor Hal a favor, because if he'd actually managed to place his lips on her, Falkor wasn't sure that he wouldn't have been inclined to murder the stupid milksop.

Falkor pondered each and every day the potential consequences of just sweeping in and claiming his mate. She was his, after all. Of that he was certain. He told himself he'd walked away that second time to make room for her baby's sire. But clearly, the man had done nothing to claim her or even help her. Sobek assured him Kessily was quite capable and her mother even more so. Sobek joked that the two human females were a formidable team.

Sobek had befriended his mate and was quite sure she would make a splendid drakaina. He had yet to discern the identity of the child's father. Kessily was exceptionally close-mouthed about it. On more than one occasion, Sobek had wondered aloud if there wasn't any way the child wasn't Falkor's, but both had quickly agreed it was impossible. Although that knowledge brought him little comfort.

He was to meet with his second-in-command later today. Nadon had stayed in Denver to offer any assistance he could to Sobek, who reported the young dragon seemed to be finding himself. Falkor stepped out onto the flat area in front of his dwelling. He called to his dragon who emerged in a burst of fire, lightning, thunder and brilliant color. Falkor roared into the sky, allowing the fire from within to spew forth as he took to the skies and headed south to Denver.

The closer he came to Denver, the more certain he was that Kessily was his eternal flame and was meant to be with him. Other dragons had been called to human mates and everything had worked out fine. He would need to wait until Kessily's child was born before turning her. He shook his head ruefully. It wasn't just Kessily's child. Regardless of its sire, it was their child—his and Kessily's. They would raise it together and when it was old enough, it would be allowed to choose its own path.

He was scheduled to meet Nadon outside of Denver shortly before dawn. Falkor hoped no one was looking too closely at his schedule or they might realize there would be a number of hours between when he left and when he met Nadon that were unaccounted for. As had been his custom since he'd left her, he flew over and around her house, keeping watch; ensuring no harm came to her.

Normally, he just kept to the sky and watched from above the clouds, but tonight, her presence called to him, and he found a secluded spot in the greenbelt behind her house where he landed and shifted. He was naked, but he didn't intend to be seen. Quietly he advanced towards her house and approached the back door.

As he had been in the house, he knew the door was not alarmed so quietly jimmied the lock and let himself into the kitchen. They'd had something Italian for dinner. He wondered if she'd ever been to Italy. She'd told him that her mother loved Paris. Maybe he'd take them all to Paris and Florence before the baby was born.

He heard moaning coming from Kessily's room and moved down the hall to ensure she was safe. What he saw when he opened the door would stay with him until his dying days. Kessily was lying on her back in her bed, her legs spread as her hands trailed down to her mons and parted her labia. He could smell and see her arousal. She'd been pleasuring herself before he'd even arrived.

Dipping her fingers into her wet heat, she brought some of it back up to rub into her swollen clit. Kessily moaned again and her toes curled as she spread her legs wider. He knew he should look away. Hell, he shouldn't be in here at all, and yet he couldn't stay away. It was all he could do not to join her in her bed. Instead, he reached down to stroke his cock. She was truly the most beautiful creature he'd ever encountered in all of his days.

Kessily rubbed her swollen nub with her index finger while parting her folds to isolate her clit and expose her pussy. A pussy he could easily remember spearing with his tongue as he made a meal of her before driving his hard rod up into her and thrusting in and out until she was screaming his name and he was filling her with his seed.

Her body spoke of her arousal—stiffened and pebbled nipples, a wet and ready pussy and her skin flushed with desire. She reached beside herself and picked up a vibrator. She brought the pulsing toy to her nub, letting it work its magic while she used her other hand to play with her breasts and nipples—rolling, pinching, and tugging. Her hips began to rock in a rhythm that was as old as time. He remembered keeping her still while he'd plundered her wet heat.

Kessily moaned as she moved the tip of the vibrator from her clit to the opening of her core and eased it inside. He could well recall the exquisite feeling of stretching her with the broad head of his cock, before pressing himself inside her. Each time had been more incredible than the last, including when he'd impaled her with his shaft in the elevator.

The way her entire body had trembled as her pussy had clamped down on him, quivering up and down his length, was something he would never forget and one in which he planned to indulge the rest of his life.

She worked the toy in and out as she further stimulated her clit. He remembered the way she'd squealed as he'd thrust into her, hitting her clit each time he surged forward, Kessily closed her eyes and tossed her head back and forth as her body stiffened in anticipation of her oncoming climax. She increased the speed with which she fucked herself until her orgasm crashed over her, and she called his name before her body became languorous with satisfaction.

It wouldn't be long, he vowed silently, until she had no need for toys or self-stimulation. He would take care of that for her. He would ride her long, hard, and often, making her come repeatedly before emptying himself into her as she writhed beneath him.

Falkor withdrew. If he'd had any doubts as to where her heart and soul lay, he had heard his answer when she called out to him. Silently he left her house and retreated to the woods. She would not have to wait for long.

The Phantom Fire kept a townhouse in Denver for business and other purposes. Sobek and Nadon were there. He had arranged for Nadon to meet him outside the city in a remote location with clothing where Falkor could land, shift, dress and then head into the city.

"Greetings, Alpha," called the young dragon when Falkor landed.

Falkor shifted and took the clothes and boots Nadon had brought for him. "Thank you. Sobek tells me you have proved very useful and have often willingly taken on more responsibilities than we had thought you were capable of."

"My father was a great warrior and served the Phantom Fire for more than five centuries. I do not intend to disgrace him."

"I think there's little chance of that," said Falkor, getting into the back of the SUV.

Falkor smiled as he remembered shifting back from human to dragon and flying up into the mountains that surrounded Denver. It had taken a frigid, towering waterfall to take the edge off his hard-on. He would forego any pleasure from his own hand until he had her once again, and then it would be Kessily who supplied him with all the pleasure he needed.

When they reached the townhouse, Falkor tossed

Nadon a one-hundred-dollar bill, telling him to go buy himself the best breakfast he could find.

Sobek lifted an eyebrow. "You have things to say to me you don't want the wyvern to hear?"

"He's more than a wyvern, and you know it. He is his father's son at the same age."

Sobek nodded. "That doesn't change the fact that you want to speak to me alone without worrying about anyone else overhearing."

"I do. What have you found out about the man who sired Kessily's child?"

"Not much. It's kind of a delicate situation. I don't think that anyone other than her mother and her doctor even know about the pregnancy. I'm often amazed at how human males can't scent the changes in their mate when her womb is ripe with life. But that's neither here nor there. I can't just ask her directly, as I can't very well explain how I know."

"I can't believe a man would turn his back on her for any reason, much less when she carries his child."

"I agree. I do know one thing, though…"

"What's that?" asked Falkor as he moved around the well-appointed living room.

"She pines for you." Falkor snorted. "Deny it all you like, but I've seen her. There's a sadness there that even the baby can't compensate for."

"Maybe it's the baby's father…"

"No, it's you. She's a very clever lawyer, your mate. She asks questions about you all the time, but only ones that are legitimate to ask. She doesn't want to seem as though she misses you. With regard to the case, we'll be moving up to the venue later this week. If you're so keen to find the name of the man whose seed took your place, ask her."

"She wasn't inclined to tell me when I did."

"From what she's let slip, you didn't ask, you accused. And that's the issue."

"I what?"

Sobek chuckled. "I'm not quite sure what you said, but regardless of what you *said*, what she *heard* was that you thought she'd been sleeping around."

"I did no such thing. I asked about who it might be as I knew for damn sure it wasn't me."

"What is it Shakespeare said? 'There are more things in Heaven and Earth, Horatio, than are dreamt of in your philosophy.'"

"This isn't philosophy; it's a fact. A dragon can't impregnate a human female."

"But it is. There is a philosophy that says you can't be the sire. There's a philosophy that says if you choose to mate with your eternal flame, you must give up your immortality, leave the Phantom Fire, and relinquish your first-born son to the brotherhood."

"Your point being?"

"That maybe after thousands of years, we might want to rethink a lot of our philosophies. I can't imagine anyone at the head of the Phantom Fire except you."

"I will not give her up."

"And no one's asking you to. Where did this tradition begin, anyway? Was it decreed by the gods, or did we, ourselves, commit it to action and memory? Let's begin a new tradition, one where if the warrior in question chooses to stay, we take a vote and let him. And maybe it's time we expanded our ranks by allowing others to join us who wish to."

Looking into Sobek's face, for the first time, Falkor saw a different way… a different life, one in which he could have Kessily and all of their children, and yet did not have to sacrifice his service to the Phantom Fire.

It was… mind-blowing.

CHAPTER 15

KESSILY

orning. Ugh. Well at least she was no longer waking each morning with incredible nausea and a need to empty the contents of her stomach into the toilet. That was a definite plus.

It might have been a better morning except for the whole can't-sleep-because-of-sex-dreams-of-Falkor thing. The dreams had taken a curious turn. At first, the dreams had simply been reliving the past. Now they seemed to lay out a possible future with the father of her child. The odd part was in almost every dream she could hear the roar of a dragon and see one flying high overhead. Kessily should have found that disconcerting; instead, she found it oddly comforting. But as much as she might have liked to stay in bed, she had a busy morning ahead of her.

On the agenda for today was a meeting with Sobek to talk about what came next in the lawsuit against Firedrake. They were ready to move from Denver up to Wyoming, as the trial was going to start with some preliminary hearings. First up would be a cease-and-desist order to stop Firedrake from clear-cutting the land in order to begin preparing the area for their casino and resort. They'd held a Zoom hearing and the judge's clerk had indicated the judge was ready to sign the actual document. The plan was for her and Sobek to fly up this afternoon and have it signed. After that they would serve it, both on Fire-drake as well as having a messenger deliver one to Bruce Chapman in New York.

Picking up the bag she had packed the previous evening, Kessily walked into the kitchen, took one look at her mother and knew she would be traveling to Wyoming alone. "If you feel half as bad as you look, I don't think you should come to Wyoming—at least not today."

Her mother's smile was one of sheer grit and determination. "I hope I do look better than I feel. I think that damn Millie managed to pass along her germs to the rest of us. When I talked to Becky last night, she said she had a fever and a headache." Kessily approached her mother, who stuck her arms out in front of her. "No. Keep your distance. Virtual hugs only."

Kessily smiled. "You stay home and take care of yourself. I'll have some chicken soup and other goodies delivered by the deli so at most all you have to do is reheat them."

"Thank you, sweetheart. Are you and Sobek going to serve them today with the cease and desist? I think he's the nicest man, don't you?"

"I do and stop what you're thinking. I have no time for a relationship with any man, much less one I have to work with. So, stop playing matchmaker."

"He's good looking and quite charming."

"And his best friend is Falkor."

"You really liked him—Falkor, I mean."

Kessily nodded. "The operative word being 'liked' as in past tense. His outright rejection of even the possibility of his being the father and then accusing me of sleeping around put a stop to that. No; this baby and I don't need that jerk in our lives."

She grabbed some breakfast, blew her mother a kiss, and headed out. Once she was at the Sierra Club's headquarters, she met with her boss, Clancy, and Sobek, who seemed to have figured out that she was pregnant and was always solicitous of her condition without giving anything away to her colleagues. It was one of the things she appreciated about him. She also admired both his loyalty to his friend and his sharp and inquisitive mind.

After Clancy left the meeting and she was putting her papers into her briefcase, Sobek touched her arm. "How are you feeling?" he asked.

"Better. The morning sickness seems to have passed."

"That's good. I took the liberty of having your assistant cancel your flight. We have a private plane. I thought you'd be more comfortable. And if you like, you can leave your car here, and I'll have our driver take us out to the plane."

Normally that kind of thing would have annoyed her but knowing that Sobek was truly only trying to be kind, she smiled. "Thank you. That would be nice."

"Then if you're ready to go, we can be off."

"That would be great. That'll give me a chance to get settled in."

They headed down to the parking garage and were picked up by Sobek's driver and SUV. It was nice just to settle back and let him arrange things. Once on board the jet, it was an easy, smooth flight to Angel Falls, Wyoming, the town closest to the property in dispute as well as the location of one of Firedrake's satellite offices. Normally that might worry Kessily, but she'd found the company and its people hadn't made a lot of friends, bringing in workers from outside the area.

When they touched down, there was an SUV waiting and Sobek drove the two of them to the courthouse where they presented their order. Chapman had yet to arrive but was virtually present.

"Once again your honor, I strenuously object," Chapman said.

"I understand that, Counselor, and your objection is noted for the record, but I will not have this wilderness destroyed before the outcome of the trial is known."

Chapman quieted down, and the order was signed.

"Mr. Chapman, a copy of the signed order will be delivered to you before the end of business today," Kessily said. She turned to Sobek. "Let's go serve Mr. Sarkany with these papers, and then I'll get set up in the Airbnb my mother arranged."

"Are you sure you don't want to stay in the hotel? It's very nice, and there is a two-bedroom suite for when your mother joins you. She is coming, isn't she?" asked Sobek.

"Yes. She's just caught some nasty flu virus. It's probably better if we aren't sharing the same space, and I really like the place she found. I ordered some things from our local deli—they have a great selection of food. It'll be delivered later today."

"I'm sorry to hear she isn't feeling well. Why don't you let me have Nadon pick up the things from the deli and deliver them. He can make sure she's doing all right and keep an eye on her for you."

"I should probably tell you it isn't necessary, but I would really appreciate that."

"Think nothing of it," Sobek assured her. "Now let's go beard the dragon in his own den."

She kind of liked the gleeful expression that came over Sobek's face whenever they were going to do something they knew would annoy Warren Sarkany— she felt the exact same way. They drove out to the property where Sarkany had already started clearing the land.

"Mr. Sarkany?"

Sarkany turned around and scowled. "What do you two want? Chapman told me he lost this battle and that the judge signed your cease and desist order."

"Yes, but serving you personally is so much more fun," said Kessily with a grin. She really shouldn't be enjoying this as much as she was. She held out the signed order. "Warren Sarkany, you've been served. By order of Judge Chutkan, you are hereby ordered to cease and desist any and all preparation and/or construction on the property in question."

"That means, Sarkany, you have to turn off your machines and send your men home."

"This will never hold up," blustered an enraged Sarkany.

"The cease and desist?" asked Kessily. "I think you'll find it does. I doubt Chapman will even want to file for an appeal. He did register his objection with the Court, but with the old growth issues and some of the other environmental concerns, he'll never win. He knows that. Not having an environmental impact statement is about to come back and bite you in the ass."

"You bitch," Sarkany snarled as he took a step forward, only to be blocked by Sobek.

"I think you'll find the court takes a dim view of one of its people being threatened or attacked," said Sobek.

"You can't stop progress," Sarkany said to Kessily before turning on Sobek. "And you'll find you can't stop me."

"Go blow fire up your ass," returned Sobek, who seemed on the verge of a physical altercation.

Kessily laid her hand on his arm. "He isn't worth it. He won't win. He can bluster and threaten all he wants, but in the end, we will prevail."

"You'd better be careful, bitch. This isn't over, not by a long shot."

Kessily turned back to him—there was a feral rage there, and she was sure that if he'd been able to breathe fire like the dragons in *Game of Thrones*, she'd have been charred to a crisp and then would have crumbled to the ground in ashes. Apparently, losing wasn't a normal occurrence in Sarkany's life.

"I'm going to let that threat slide. I'm telling you, and I will tell your lawyer, if there's a next time, I won't be so understanding. Sobek is correct, Judge Chutkan takes these kinds of things seriously and won't hesitate to toss your ass in jail for the duration of the trial. As this is to be a lengthy process, you might want to think about that."

Sobek escorted her back to the SUV and headed back towards town to pick up her clothing so Sobek could deliver her to her home for the next few months.

"Are you sure you want to stay in that place you rented? It's awfully isolated. I know Falkor would like it better if you were in town at the hotel."

"What your buddy Falkor wants or doesn't want ceased to matter to me when he accused me of being a slut."

"He never did that…"

"He might not have used the word, but he certainly implied it."

"You're sure there is no chance the father could be anyone but Falkor."

"The only candidate for the father of my unborn child—whether he likes it or not—is Falkor."

Kessily placed her hand on her belly and looked out the window. Why did it have to hurt so much when Sobek brought up Falkor? Why couldn't she just accept what a bastard he was and move on.

"He cares about you."

"He doesn't," she argued. "Everything he has done since he found out I was carrying his child speaks to how much of an asshole he really is."

"I can tell you more than one of our men has asked about who Falkor is pining away for. He only eats enough to sustain him, but he trains harder than anyone, and when he doesn't think anyone is looking, there is a haunted, hollow look that threatens to consume him."

"Men?" she asked. "Train?"

Sobek nodded. "There is a group of us who served in the same special ops unit. When we came back, we bought some land and formed a kind of commune where we all live and work together. Falkor likes to keep in shape, and we have an excellent gym facility in the common area."

"Sounds interesting. I guess I pictured him on a palatial estate."

"Far from it," Sobek chuckled. "We have individual dwellings that resemble upgraded yurts."

In some ways she had an easier time picturing him in something like Sobek described as opposed to a mansion with finely manicured lawns and a tennis court.

"I'm not convinced he's 'pining away' for any girl," said Kessily, "but if he is, I'm quite sure the feeling is not reciprocal."

"I know you don't want to hear any of this, but I have you captive in my SUV, so you have to sit and listen. I can't do anything about whether or not you will choose to hear me. But Falkor is one of the finest men I've ever known. He has faced and conquered challenges you can't even imagine. He has triumphed in the face of overwhelming odds and has always treated those around him with kindness and caring. Did he fuck up when you told him about the pregnancy? Of course, he did, but maybe it was because he'd let his guard slip with you and what the two of you shared was something he's never experienced or expected."

Sobek sounded so sincere, and maybe all of that was true, but she hadn't deserved his accusations and sure as hell hadn't deserved his abandonment. More to the point, neither did their baby.

No, she would win this case and put a stop to Sarkany's resort and casino, and then she would figure out how she and her child would make the best lives possible for themselves—Falkor be damned.

CHAPTER 16

FALKOR

Falkor was waiting at the hotel—at first in the bar, and then he had paced the floor of the hotel lobby. He couldn't believe Sobek had let her just blithely walk into danger like that when they'd served Sarkany personally. What was he thinking? And where the fuck was the father of her baby? Did he care nothing for either of them? He could understand if it was a one-night stand, how a man might not want to be tied to a woman he didn't love, but how could he just abandon his child? Did he even know about the baby?

She and Sobek entered the hotel. One look at him and the expression on her face turned from laughing and carefree to stoney and sullen. She was pissed at him? By what right did she think she was entitled to feel that? It didn't matter; he'd made the decision to forgive her transgression and the two of them would raise the child together, perhaps at Dragonwyk. Sobek had not been the only one to talk to him about whether or not continuing to cleave to the old ways might not be in the Phantom Fire's best interest.

Kessily picked up her bag and then turned to head back outside.

Falkor stepped in front of her, halting her progress.

"Move," she said with barely contained hostility.

"No. You and I need to talk."

"No, we don't. I don't have anything more to say to you, and you don't have anything to say that I care to hear."

Grasping her arm, he marched her into a corner of the lobby.

"Let go of me," she said, jerking her arm away. "I don't want to make a scene, so say whatever it is you have to say and then get out of my way."

"I've been doing a lot of thinking. It doesn't matter who the father of your baby is. Whoever he is, he is unworthy of you."

"You got that right," she sneered.

The vehemence of her anger took Falkor by surprise. He hadn't expected her to agree with him quite so easily or to be as angry as she was. Although considering the bastard had deserted her, he could understand that.

"In any event, I've decided it doesn't matter. I am

willing to overlook your past indiscretion as we weren't together…"

"You're willing? My indiscretion?" she seethed. "You arrogant bastard. The only indiscretion I've had in the past few years is you. Do you hear that? You." She put her finger in his chest and poked. "I'm going to tell you for the last time. There is one, and only one, candidate for the father of my baby. That would be you. And if you think I'll let you near my baby at this point, you are sadly mistaken. You don't want to be a part of our lives? Good. We don't want you. Now get out of my way." She called past him to Sobek, "The rental company is bringing my SUV. I'll wait for it outside. This lobby is making me ill."

Falkor was taken aback to the point where she was able to push past him and head outside to the SUV she had rented and arranged to have delivered to her at the hotel. He hadn't wanted to upset her. He looked at Sobek, who merely shrugged as if to say, 'you're on your own.'

Unable to vent his spleen on her, he turned it on Sobek. "What the fuck was that about? And why the hell did you let her confront Sarkany in person? You let her get right up in his face. Those men who were working are members of his clan. He could have burned both of you to a crisp and mixed your ashes into the concrete."

It was Sobek's turn to be outraged. "You were

watching us? Since when don't you trust me to take care of the Phantom Fire's business?"

"I wasn't checking up on you. I wanted to have your back, just in case." Falkor shook his head. Sobek had a right to be angry. "She is my eternal flame. My thoughts are not rational where she is concerned. That confrontation between them could have turned deadly."

"But it didn't, nor would I have allowed it to. She was never in danger. Never. I would have given my life to protect your eternal flame and your child."

"My child… there's no way."

"There must be. She is pregnant, and she swears there has been no one else but you. I, for one, believe her. I can't explain how it happened, but it did. You insulted her integrity and honor; then, in her mind, ran when she mentioned the word pregnant. I think you may find her righteous indignation a far more ruthless opponent than the Cherufe."

He could see the truth of the matter on Sobek's face. Falkor's anger deflated like a balloon pricked by a pin. "Shit." From her point of view, he had done nothing right since she'd told him she was pregnant. What a slap in the face his accusations must have been, but how could she be pregnant with his child? It was impossible—or was it? Could she be telling the truth?

It came to him with shattering clarity that even if it wasn't possible; even if he wasn't the one who supplied the seed to her egg, she was telling him her truth. She absolutely believed that she was carrying his child. And if she could believe, why the hell couldn't he?

He looked up to see her standing on the sidewalk waiting for the car rental agency to deliver her vehicle. He needed to talk to her; needed to make her understand he knew how wrong he'd been. Wasn't the level of her anger an indicator that she loved him or at least cared for him? He could see an SUV approaching. He needed to stop her from getting in that SUV.

He exited the hotel and started towards her. She stepped off the curb, trying to get to the SUV. Something in his peripheral vision caught his attention and he saw the moment the approaching SUV began to accelerate, bearing down on Kessily at a blazing degree of speed.

KESSILY

How dare he tell her he was willing to forgive her *indiscretions*? The bastard refused to believe her and refused to believe he could be the father. Even if he'd had a vasectomy, there was a slim chance. The odds had certainly been stacked against them, but stranger things had happened. Why couldn't she just accept that he was an uncaring sonofabitch and move on? Would she even want him in her baby's life?

She could hear him shouting. It barely penetrated her fog of anger and hurt, but it did. She stopped to look at where the shout had come from. Just behind him there was a dark SUV moving towards her at an alarming speed and accelerating. She suddenly understood why deer often were standing stock still when they were hit. She knew she needed to move, but she couldn't seem to get her legs and feet to understand the danger. She turned her back to the car—her first thought to protect her unborn child.

Falkor moved with the grace of an apex predator, hitting her body a fraction of a second before the SUV could. With his arms wrapped around her, he engineered their fall so that his body took the brunt of the impact with the concrete. He rolled away from the curb as people began shouting and rushing around. Those who had been milling around in front of the hotel were suddenly scattered everywhere.

"Are you all right?" he said. "Please tell me you're all right."

"Other than feeling like I got hit by a freight train, I'm fine. Thank you for that. I could see the danger, but I couldn't seem to move."

"It's all right. You're safe now. We didn't fall on the baby, did we?"

"No. I had turned my back, and when you hit me, you pulled me back into your body and hit the concrete with your back. My god, Falkor, are you all right?"

"I am fine, beloved," he said pushing her hair back off her face and kissing her forehead. "Let's get you up."

"What did you just call me?" she said archly as he helped her to his feet.

"I called you beloved."

"Why would you say that?" she said trying to pull away from him, but he held tight.

"Because it is true. You have to forgive me."

"No, I don't."

"Of course, you do. I just saved your life. Surely that buys me a one-time pass on being an idiot."

He was so gorgeous, and everything in his face and body language told her he was sincere.

"Kessily, I've never begged anyone for anything in my life. But I'm begging you now to believe me that I know how wrong I was. When you said this baby was mine, I should have accepted that regardless of my understanding of how it could be true. You need to believe that I do believe and that I will never, ever abandon our baby again."

She nodded. "I swear I will cut your balls off and force them down your throat to watch you choke on them if you do."

"How could you ever doubt that in her heart, your eternal flame was already drakaina?" said Sobek as he joined them.

"Did you get a license plate?" Falkor asked.

"There wasn't one. My guess is it was recently stolen with this specific purpose in mind. It will be abandoned quickly."

"Want to tell me again how allowing her to confront Sarkany wasn't dangerous?" Falkor snarled at Sobek before Kessily punched him in the arm, making him growl at her.

"Don't you growl at me, and don't you dare be mean to Sobek. He does not control my actions any more than you do. Sarkany is a low-lying piece of shit, and I wanted to watch him squirm. This was only the first time. I promise you it won't be the last."

The sounds of people shouting and shrieking had provided cover for their conversation. As it died down, the sounds of sirens wailing in the distance could be heard.

"I would suggest, Alpha, that you get your mate to safety and let me deal with the cops."

"Hello?" said Kessily. "I'm right here, and I will tell what little I know to the cops."

"Sweetheart, it would be far better for us to deal with Sarkany than the authorities. He's a dangerous man, and his missed opportunity at killing you will not be left unresolved."

"What do you mean by that?" she asked, confused but liking the way he called her sweetheart warmed her heart and soul.

"He'll try again," the two men said in unison.

"Sobek is right. It isn't safe for you here in town. I want you and the baby where I can ensure your safety."

"She'll be needed in court each day starting Monday."

"Then we will bring her in. Didn't you say the place her mother rented was outside of town in a secluded spot?"

"You've been spying on me for him?" accused Kessily.

"Yes," they said in unison again.

"We can use it as a base. Tell Nadon he is to watch Meri and keep her safe at all costs. We will send others to help."

Sobek handed him the keys to the SUV he'd rented. "You take care of her; I will handle the authorities. I'll tell them you are concerned about the birth of your unborn child and will make her available in a day or two."

Falkor grabbed her hand and began to take them to the hotel's parking lot. Once inside the SUV, she asked him. "Where exactly are we going? That was the only nice hotel in town. Do you really think my mother is in danger?" With the shock of her near-death experience wearing off, her mind was suddenly buzzing.

"I wouldn't put it outside the realm of possibilities. Sarkany is a dangerous, violent man. I will do what is necessary to protect those who are mine."

"And that includes my mother?"

"That includes you, your mother, and our baby."

"Do you believe me? Really?"

"I believe you when you tell me you have been with no other. That means, however improbable it may be, the truth is that the child you carry is mine." As they pulled out onto the highway, Falkor used the speed dial on his phone. "Raine? I need you at Dragonwyk. It's important."

"Is it Kessily?" a feminine voice asked.

"Yes," he said a bit tersely.

Kessily was pretty sure the laughter that came over the speaker was the reason for the snarl in his voice. "This should be fun. I'll be there as quickly as I can."

"Only if Cooper allows it."

Another laugh. "Yeah. When have I ever let that stop me from doing anything I wanted? See you tomorrow."

The call ended.

"And who is Raine?" Kessily asked suspiciously.

Falkor lifted her hand to his lips and kissed it. "My sister. My obnoxious, unrelentingly badly-behaved sister. I had hoped the two of you would never meet."

Kessily grinned. "She sounds absolutely delightful. I can't wait."

Falkor rolled his eyes and groaned as he placed another call. "Zahran? I am bringing my mate to Dragonwyk. She carries my child."

Zahran. What did Falkor and his friends have against last names or first names for that matter?

"How is that possible? Didn't I hear she was human?"

Human? What the hell else would I be?

"I don't know, and yes. We had a bit of a scare, and I'd like you to look her over and make sure she and the baby are safe. Also, I don't think I left my dwelling in the best possible order."

Zahran laughed. "I will see that attended to."

"Sobek has the coordinates of where I want the chopper sent."

"I will see to that, as well."

"Thank you."

"It is always my pleasure to serve, Alpha."

Falkor ended the call.

"I have questions: Alpha. Sobek called you that as well."

Falkor nodded. "He did. It is what those of the Phantom Fire, the special ops group I served with and who now act as mercenaries when needed, call me to show respect. Trust me, you will never hear Raine call me that." He said the latter with a grin.

"And Dragonwyk?"

"That's what we call the place where we live. I'm sure you have questions and lots of them. I promise once I have you safe, I will answer anything you need or want me to."

She nodded; that was fair. Despite anything he

might have said to the contrary, it was obvious he loved his sister. He was right, her other questions could wait, but she wanted and needed to know at least a little bit more about his family. After all, they would be her baby's family too.

"Do you have other siblings?" she asked. "Are your parents still alive? How are they going to feel about some strange woman carrying their first grandchild? Wait. Do you have other children? I promise I'll hold the rest of my questions until we get to Dragonwyk, but I would appreciate some basic answers. I feel I know so little about you."

"That seems fair. I have no other siblings, other than those I call my brothers. My parents are long gone and those of us who are pledged to the brotherhood have no mate and no children. To be a part of the Phantom Fire is to vow to put it first. If you are lucky enough to have and find the one woman who completes you, you give up your place, and another rises to take it."

CHAPTER 17

FALKOR

"Is that why you didn't want the baby to be yours?" she asked in a quiet voice.

"No. God no," he said, finding a place to pull off so he could turn and face her. "I have never wanted anything more in this life than to believe the baby you carry was mine. I simply did not think there was a possibility that I…"

His sentence was cut off as a brilliant burst of flames hit the front of the windshield, melting it. Falkor was out of the SUV and over to her side, opening the door and pulling her out in what seemed like a heartbeat. "Run!" he snarled, and she offered him no argument.

The two of them charged towards the trees on the other side of the clearing. Behind them she could hear the great beating of wings, breaking the surface of the air with a thunder-like clap.

"Keep running," he shouted.

He didn't have to tell her twice. She was glad of his strong hand holding hers as he led them across the open field. The sound of the wings grew louder, and Kessily knew whatever it was behind them was gaining on them. When it was obvious that they wouldn't make the relative safety of the trees, Falkor stopped, pulling her past him and spinning her around.

"I need you to stay calm and low to the ground. There are only three of them…"

Whatever he said after that was lost on her as she spotted three gigantic dragons over his shoulder. Kessily closed her eyes and looked again. She felt light headed as if she was about to pass out, but fought down that instinct. If those were what she thought they were, fainting could get them both killed as she knew Falkor would not leave her.

She could feel her eyes widen. "D… D… Dragons," she finally managed to get out.

Falkor took a deep breath. "Yes, dragons," he said in a far too calm a voice. "Do you believe I love you?"

"I do," she said, knowing she spoke the truth, but not taking her eyes off the approaching formation of dragons.

"Remember that."

He stepped back and was immediately encased in a swirling storm cloud of lightning, thunder, fire, and color. She raised her hand to ward off the heat and bright light that emanated from the maelstrom that surrounded him. From the depths of the middle of the chaos, an enormous silver dragon arose, roaring and spewing fire into the sky.

If she'd thought she wanted to faint before, now she felt as though she wanted to throw up and then pass out. She could not believe that Falkor had somehow morphed into a dragon. That simply wasn't possible and yet she had seen him do it.

The other dragons flew toward them in a V formation. The one in the lead shrieked at them and the dragon she believed to somehow be Falkor unleashed a vortex of fire from his mouth, hitting the dragon at the front of the formation full-on, sending it up in flames as it fell from the sky.

Beating his wings, Falkor rose higher than the other dragons flew, spewing fire at them and driving them away from Kessily. She watched, fascinated. She couldn't seem to tear her eyes away or look for better cover. A small part of her brain told her to run, to put distance between herself and the great monsters that flew overhead, but it was beyond her ability to do so. She seemed frozen in space, as well as in time.

The other part shushed her and told her to sit back and not miss any of the incredible, unbelievable spectacle playing out before her. There were dragons; they were real. It was beyond her comprehension and yet here they were, and one of them was somehow the man she loved.

Overhead, one of the dragons turned back in a ploy to lead Falkor away. But he wasn't so easily fooled. He banked and came after the one who was the greater threat to her. He overtook the dragon, using his teeth to shred his opponent's wing and send him to the ground. Falkor followed him down, grasping the other's body with his razor-like claws, slashing at it as its lifeblood ran like a fast-flowing river to pool on the ground beside it.

When the creature breathed its last, Falkor rose up above the carnage and roared in triumph. The dragon who had thought to lure him away had left his comrade to face death alone. Falkor settled on the ground not too far from her and was once again encased in a storm cloud of fire, color, thunder, and lightning.

Kessily raced to his side as the maelstrom dissipated and what was left was not a dragon, but the man she loved. She stumbled a little at the thought. She wasn't sure which concept hit her harder—that she loved Falkor or that somehow, inexplicably, he was a dragon, or at least could become one.

She could see the evidence of the fight on his body, deep slashes that were bleeding freely. Kessily ran to him, tearing at her cotton skirt and binding his wounds as best she could. Overhead, she heard the shriek of more dragons. Before she could even think or react, Falkor laid a hand upon her, calming her.

"Those are my brothers. We are safe."

"That's all right then, I guess." The words had barely left her mouth when the blackness that had been threatening to overcome her since the windshield melted overwhelmed all of her senses and she slid to the ground in a dead faint.

As her mind began to clear and the darkness retreated she had a vivid recollection of the woman she'd met in the Winds.

Kessily had withdrawn a card from the old woman's deck.

"You chose the silver dragon of imagination, possibility, and self-discovery," the woman had said.

The card had depicted a large silver dragon flying over the peaks of the Winds.

"What are you trying to tell me?" Kessily had asked.

The old woman's prophecy came to mind: "It is not I who speaks to you, but the dragon lord who will claim you."

When she woke, Falkor was beside her.

"What the proverbial fuck?" she asked, making him chuckle.

"I'm sorry, sweetheart. Did I forget to mention I was a human-dragon shifter?"

"It must have just slipped your mind," she said sarcastically.

"Yes, that must be it."

She reached out her hand to trace new scars on his body that hadn't been there before. Scars that corresponded to the wounds she had seen on him before she passed out.

"I fainted. I never faint," she said.

"I think it's understandable. My guess is you've never seen dragons before or learned that one had sired your baby or seen them in battle."

Truer words had never been spoken. She was glad to know at least they had won the battle, but she had a nasty feeling that the war had just begun.

"The baby," she said feeling her small bump.

"Zahran says both of you are fine. I had him examine you, and even had Sobek bring up an ultrasound."

"But how?"

"I asked Zahran the same question, and his explanation came down to life finds a way."

"Is Sobek a dragon?"

"Technically a dragon-shifter, but yes, as are Nadon, my sister, Zahran, and all of those who comprise the Phantom Fire."

"Is that why none of you have last names?"

"Yes. The Phantom Fire are an ancient sect of warriors…"

"Who battled the Cherufe and banded together to keep the world safe…" said a woman in a melodramatic voice. Kessily turned to see a woman standing across the room just inside the doorway.

"Raine, that is enough," said Falkor with a scowl.

"Don't blame me; blame your other sister."

"I thought you said you only had one sister," said Kessily completely confused. "And Cherufe?"

"That's kind of complicated," said the woman

called Raine. "There are two of us, but we share a body. I used to be human until Zaphira, his original sister, needed a human host. I got elected. Now he has to deal with both of us. And the Cherufe are an even older group of bad guys that we defeated here on the surface and drove back into the bowels of the Earth."

"That is actually now Cooper's job," said Falkor.

"Cooper would be my mate," explained Raine. "Let's save the whole two souls/one body explanation for later. So, you're my big brother's eternal flame."

Kessily shook her head a little. It felt like she was swimming through a very murky pond. Nothing was clear, and the further she went, the less clear things seemed. "Eternal flame?"

Raine shook her head, her dark hair cascading all around her. "It is the dragon term for a fated mate or soul mate. We believe there is one soul in all the universe that can complete us. Unfortunately for you, yours is my butthead brother."

"Raine, that is enough," said a tall, broad-shouldered man as he entered what appeared to be, for all intents and purposes, the yurt they were in.

Raine grinned at her. "And unfortunately for me, that one is mine. Look, I think Falkor probably wanted me to come answer questions for you, but let me save you some worry: you're not a dragon yet, my niece or nephew will be born human, and he or she will be a dragon/human hybrid. I'm going to leave the whole immortality and Phantom Fire up to you," she said looking pointedly at her brother.

"Come along, Raine. Your brother's mate has been through an ordeal. She needs to rest."

"Which is Cooper-speak for he wants to get me into bed."

"Raine," both Cooper and Falkor growled.

Raine just laughed, clearly not intimidated in the least. "We'll be around a few days. If you want to talk or have questions, just come find me. Usually I'm with tall, dark, and brooding here."

Raine scampered past the imposing Cooper who swatted her backside affectionately. Kessily looked to Falkor, who groaned.

"Scoot over," he said, and she did so, lifting the covers so he could join her. He made a comfortable place for himself and then pulled her close, her head resting on his chest.

"What did she mean by 'yet?'"

"If you choose, you can go through a transition and become a dragon shifter."

"Really? You mean I could fly and breathe fire?"

"Yes, but the transition is not without its dangers, and it wouldn't be safe to do until after the baby is born."

"What about immortality? Wait a minute—how old are you?"

"Old. Very old. So old, there are parts of my ancient past I will never remember. When one of the

Phantom Fire finds his eternal mate and leaves us, he gives up his immortality. Just as when another joins us, he is granted immortality."

"Do you have to do that? I mean, if you choose me do you give up all this?"

He nodded. "But there has been a lot of talk of late that perhaps we should rethink how we do things. I know many of my men would be happier if they were allowed to take a mate."

"How do you choose new members?"

"I need you to understand that whatever happens, it will not impact our child. I never knew until now what we were asking of those who left."

"What were you asking?"

"That the firstborn son of the one who left was pledged to the Phantom Fire and joined us when he was of age."

"Are you kidding me? That's not even legal."

Falkor chuckled. "Legal isn't something dragons necessarily concern themselves with. But that is part of what we are talking about changing. Originally there were twelve of us, and all but I are descendants of the original twelve."

"Are you one of the original twelve?" she whispered.

"Yes, but I will not give up our child, regardless of what the brotherhood decides."

"And your immortality?"

"That I would give up gladly. I'm tired, but more

than that, I do not think I could live without you. I would choose a mortal life with you for however long that may be over an eternity without you."

"What happens now?"

"You win your trial, we have the baby—or rather you give birth while I stand around scared to death and look terrified."

She laughed.

"There will come a day when I will want to claim you as my eternal flame, and you can choose to become a drakaina or not. I will leave that up to you, but I will tell you the fact that you are pregnant is damn close to a miracle. Should you choose to transition, whatever human condition that prevents you from conceiving will be healed."

"So, we could have more children?" He nodded, and she smiled. "Then I choose drakaina."

"After the baby is born we will talk more about that. But for now, know that I burn bright enough for us both and if you remain human—even if we cannot have other children—I will be content. I love you, Kessily. You belong to and with me. We belong to each other, now and forever."

Falkor rolled Kessily to her back and was happy to hear her sigh of contentment. He moved down the bed until he settled himself at the apex of her thighs, lifting each leg over his back. She was deliciously, gloriously naked, just as he'd imagined her so many times. He tickled her pussy with his tongue, before drawing it up to swirl around her clit. Kessily moaned and writhed.

"You should know, pregnant women are usually incredibly horny from right about now all the way into their third trimester."

"Good to know," he teased. "I suspect we can do better than that."

He began licking, sucking and nipping her, breathing in her intoxicating scent and tasting the sweet, warm, wild honey that flowed freely. As he suckled her clit, he eased a finger inside her, groaning as he did so and remembering what it felt like to have his cock deep inside her. A second finger joined the first, and Kessily's moans became more frantic as her pleasure and need escalated.

It took no time at all to send her over the edge, calling his name as her pussy clamped down on his fingers and her honey coated his fingers. Her legs dug into his back, urging him closer. Falkor replaced his fingers with his tongue, spearing her rhythmically and feasting on her much the way a starving man would an endless buffet.

"Falkor," she moaned as he worked his way back up her body, burying his face in the valley between her breasts.

"I'm going to have to make it clear to our children that these beauties are only on loan while they have to have them," he growled, rolling her nipples between his thumb and forefinger.

He hovered over her, his hips cradled by her thighs and his upper body resting on his elbows. He slid his cock forward and back against her slick sex, getting it lubricated while all the while increasing her arousal.

Falkor eased into her in slow, shallow thrusts, pulling back only to push forward. "I've never fucked a pregnant woman before… well, not knowingly."

Kessily laughed and arched her back, trying to take more of him. "Please, Falkor, I need you."

"You have me, beloved. I will never give you cause to think otherwise again."

She sighed happily and he pushed deeper, enjoying the way she wriggled beneath him. He pulled back and then thrust deep, driving himself to the end of her core, making her gasp and claw at his back. She might never choose to transition, but his eternal flame was all drakaina.

He could feel and almost see the tether that connected them spring into place. He could feel the hum of her body beneath his as he began to move within her, drawing himself back only to plunge forward in a way that made her gasp.

Falkor held her ass in his hands to steady her and to keep her from trying to wrest control away from him, but still her hips undulated in perfect harmony with his stroking. He had started slowly and as gently as he could at this time, but that control was escaping as he began pounding into her—his feral need to go harder, faster, and deeper taking over him.

He sent her over the edge, waves of pleasure crashing all around him, making his blood sing and remember what it was to be truly alive. Kessily's body tightened around him, and she called his name again as his own orgasm washed over him, creating a cascade of spiraling pleasure as he filled her with his seed. He let himself rest on her, not giving her his full weight.

Rolling off her, Falkor pulled her close, happier and more content than he'd ever been in his very long life.

CHAPTER 18

The next few days were spent between last minute preparation for trial and settling into her new life with Falkor. They'd called her mother who was ecstatic to hear they had settled their differences and were committed to being together and to raising this and hopefully other children together.

Falkor had her mother brought up to the Airbnb where she was being watched over by Sobek and Nadon. They had explained the near miss with the SUV and that Falkor wasn't comfortable with Kessily anywhere other than his estate in the mountains. When Kessily described it as primitive living—which wasn't the case at all—her mother had chosen the luxury Airbnb.

"Why would he live like that?" asked her mother.

"Because this is an old special ops unit, and some of them just aren't comfortable around people they don't know. They prefer a more hands-on, rugged existence so they got this piece of land and all live in yurts."

"Are you happy?"

"Very, and I'll be down soon and then will be in town daily."

"How will you make the trip? Won't it be a long drive?"

"No. They have a helicopter."

"Oh, how fun. Well enjoy each other, and I'm so glad you found your way back to one another. He just seemed so perfect for you."

"He is. We are perfect for one another."

There were still things to be decided, chief among them, whether Falkor would continue as leader of the Phantom Fire, if he would give up his immortality, if Kessily would become drakaina, where they would live, and what information they would share with her mother. Those very same arguments were debated around the great bonfire every night. Kessily was impressed with the passion of those on both sides. The chief argument seemed to center around tradition versus enticing Falkor to remain as their alpha. He had a wealth of knowledge and experience that could not be duplicated.

Sobek sought her out one evening. "I got word that Sarkany…"

"Am I wrong in assuming he's also a dragon?"

"No, you are not. I've heard that Firedrake has

been secretly violating the cease-and-desist order—at night, and just a little at a time."

"We can tell the court that, but we're going to need evidence to back that up. I can request a hearing on the matter."

"I'll let your mother know. She's dying to see you but is happy you're with the alpha. Falkor is going to want someone with you at all times. Sarkany is a dragon, and he is not going to play nice. It's got to stick in his craw that not only did they miss killing you twice, but that Falkor took out two of his best warriors."

"Sobek is right," Falkor said, wrapping his arms around her as he joined them. "He is not likely to play nice, and human rules and laws mean little to nothing to him."

They were driving her nuts, the whole lot of them. If she'd thought her mother was bad, it was nothing compared to the overbearing dominance of those Falkor insisted she have with her at all times if he couldn't be there himself. There were other Phantom Fire matters he needed to attend to. In addition, he was doing some sleuthing on his own regarding Sarkany and his land development company. It appeared that the planned casino and resort was just one small piece in a much larger puzzle.

Kessily had been wanting to sneak up to the Fire-drake site to see what she could see when no one was around. The dragons that surrounded her were none too happy with that idea, and Falkor had flat out forbidden it. She smiled as she thought of his sister, Raine, saying her mate forbidding her something didn't necessarily mean she wouldn't do it.

The chance to slip away one day came after a long day of jury selection. Bruce Chapman knew his business; they'd been at it all day, but both were using up their preemptory challenges in *voir dire* at about the same rate. When the rest of the team had headed to the café for a drink, Kessily had excused herself to use the restroom and discovered a back door leading out of the café. She adored Falkor and his men, but they were a bit overbearing, and she was beginning to feel a bit suffocated.

She found one of the SUVs they'd rented, started it up, and headed up to the site. She figured she'd have the place to herself and could photograph and log the photos for evidence. It was a pleasant, late afternoon and she looked around, shaking her head. How could anyone want to destroy the pristine beauty of the site? She found plenty of evidence that they had already begun doing so in some places.

Kessily could feel his presence before he called her name.

She turned to face him with a bright smile.

"Hello, my beloved. What brings you out here? I thought you'd be with your men and my mother."

"I'm sure you did. I'm also sure I was quite clear that you were not to go off gallivanting around on your own."

"I am not gallivanting. I am gathering evidence. See all those downed trees and the tracks from the bulldozers and big trucks? We have a cease-and-desist order. All of this is in violation. I want to present it to the judge tomorrow. I just need to get a little closer to some of the trees so we can prove they were recently felled."

"You stay here by the SUV where the ground is more stable. I'll go get what you need."

"Thank you, sweetheart."

"I wouldn't be so quick to thank me. You and I are not finished talking about this."

She was leaning against the front of the SUV when she felt a rush of air accompanied by the sound of beating wings and heard Falkor shouting her name. Kessily turned to see a dragon bearing down on her. Before she could drop to the ground and roll under the vehicle, the thing wrapped its claws around her, snatching her from the ground and trying to take to the skies.

Terror silenced her. She tried to scream, but no sound came. The dragon that had her in his clutches was rapidly rising in the sky. From below, she could see the powerful maelstrom that she knew to be

Falkor's shifting from man to dragon. She could feel him reaching out to her along the tether that had recently linked them, telling her that all would be well. Even though she was dangling from the claws of a dragon, she closed her eyes briefly to calm her racing heart, forcing herself to believe him.

The dragon holding her in his grasp continued to fly higher and higher, as if he was trying to reach the sun. He circled around once, screeching into the bright blue sky high above the clouds, breathing fire before turning her loose and letting her fall.

Kessily windmilled her arms, trying to do something, though what she wasn't sure. Instinct told her to turn over so she could see where she was going, but somehow the idea of watching as impact with the Earth and death came rushing up to meet her did not have a lot of appeal.

"Still your mind and breathe. I will have you safe within my grasp in moments." She could not hear his voice but could hear him soothing her along the tether.

Almost as fast as she heard him, she felt the loving talons of her immortal beloved wrap around her.

"I have you."

"I know—now and forever. I never doubted you."

Falkor took her back to the SUV. "Get inside and stay there."

Within the blink of an eye, he was flying back into the air in pursuit of the dragon that had snatched and then dropped her. Kessily didn't like that dragon's odds of survival against her eternal flame.

~

FALKOR

Seeing Sarkany snatch Kessily from the ground had not only made his heart begin to hammer in his chest, but it had slowed time and space to a crawl. He could feel her sense of calm and love coming back down the tether when he reached out to her to reassure her he was coming. Nothing had ever felt better. He would not let her down, and Sarkany, as he knew the dragon to be, would not survive a third attempt on his mate's life.

His heart had damn near stopped when Sarkany circled and then dropped her, knowing full well that Falkor would do anything to save her. He was surprised that Sarkany hadn't come screaming out of the skies to engage in battle when Falkor caught her. Instead, he had circled overhead as Falkor placed her on the ground.

Beating his wings to ascend into the clouds and beyond, Falkor roared with rage and allowed the air to be split by his call. If anyone heard him, he didn't care. This was the business of dragons. Sarkany came soaring through the clouds, his massive teeth snapping as he tried to ambush Falkor. But Sarkany was young, and he was mortal—the two things Falkor was not.

Falkor banked hard, catching Sarkany's wing and sending the wyvern somersaulting through the sky— as that's how he thought of him: young, inexperienced, and destined never to be anything else. He wouldn't live that long. His lover's fear for Kessily and their unborn child was gone, replaced with the long-honed focus of a warrior.

He dove towards the Earth, dropping beneath Sarkany, then reversing his flight so that he came back underneath him, sinking his teeth into Sarkany's soft belly. Sarkany roared with rage and pain. Falkor tore a chunk of his underside away, then spat out the flesh and blood of his opponent. It was the ultimate insult: Sarkany was not fit to consume.

Only to destroy.

Sarkany slashed at Falkor with his claws, and Falkor banked away and out of his grasp, plunging toward the Earth to pick up speed in order to swoop back up and attack Sarkany again. This time his enemy saw him coming and leveled off on a direct collision course.

They slammed into each other, each sinking his teeth into the other's neck while their claws slashed and grappled with each other. Their wings were too close to the other to beat properly, the ouroboros of their entwined forms spiraling toward certain death below. Falkor tucked his wings—in this instance they were more of a hindrance than a help—and increased the velocity with which they tumbled toward certain death.

Realizing the end of his life was near, Sarkany released his hold on Falkor, probably hoping Falkor would do the same. That thought had never entered his mind. Instead, Falkor spread his wings and released Sarkany for only an instant before flying above him and sinking his claws into Sarkany's back just over where his wings joined his body, rendering them useless.

With lethal intent, Falkor flew towards one of the craggy peaks, intent on smashing Sarkany into the rocks and ensuring he never bothered anyone again. His opponent struggled and screeched in dread and fury, but Falkor would not relinquish his hold. With deliberate intent to make his enemy suffer, one at a time he shredded each of Sarkany's wings. Now, even if Sarkany could find a way to make Falkor release him, he would fall to his death.

But Falkor would not give him that luxury, not give him that boon. Sarkany would die knowing full well it was happening, his wings destroyed and his opponent's claws holding him prisoner as he drove him into the side of the mountain.

Falkor thrust Sarkany at the cliff face, releasing him just as he hit the rock with a tremendous crack, like the sound of thunder, which drowned at his death cries. There was a cascade of blood and scales as the sky and the mountain both vibrated with the horror of Sarkany's death.

Falkor flew back to Kessily. This might be their undoing. She had seen dragons at their best, but how would she handle them at their worst? As he approached the SUV, he could see Kessily surrounded by Sobek and Nadon.

Falkor landed and shifted from dragon to man. Before he could take the towel from Sobek to try and remove some of the blood and other bits of Sarkany from his body, Kessily had flung herself into his arms.

"That was the scariest, most incredible thing I ever saw. Are you all right? You're not hurt? Well, you're probably hurt, but nothing fatal, right?" The words tumbled out of her.

Figuring the best way to reassure her and quiet her at the same time was to kiss her, Falkor fused his mouth to hers, thrusting his tongue past her lips and letting her feel the passion and victory coursing through his blood. Finally, he lifted his mouth but kept his arms around her.

"You saw where I ended him?"

"Yes, Alpha," answered Sobek.

"I want you both to go up there and reduce him to ashes. Sprinkle them here on this place he sought to destroy and let what remains of him nourish the earth."

Both Nadon and Sobek shifted and took to the sky

as Falkor wiped the blood from his body before taking the clothes Kessily handed to him.

"You're not disgusted?" he asked, half-afraid of her answer.

"Not even one bit. If any bastard ever deserved a nasty death, it was him. I will say, however, you give the term eco-warrior a whole new meaning."

Falkor chuckled, pulled on the clothes and then helped her into the SUV. "The two of them can take the other two SUVs back. What happens with Sarkany's death?"

"His company is a sole proprietorship, so it'll have to go through probate. The site will most likely be put up for sale, and the Sierra Club will try to raise funds to buy it."

Falkor shook his head. "The Phantom Fire is wealthy beyond your wildest imaginings. We'll buy it and ensure it is never threatened again."

Falkor now stood where he had seen so many before him do the same to take their eternal flame to mate. Only now, the ceremony had fundamentally changed. No longer would a warrior of the Phantom Fire be forced to choose between honor and duty and the woman or drakaina he loved. Instead, if asked and if they chose to, they would remain at Dragonwyk to serve as one of the elite warriors and have a family.

Zahran raised his arms.

"Today marks the first of a new age of the Phantom Fire. Our great leader, Falkor, has been gifted with his eternal flame. It is obvious from her growing belly…" there was much good-natured laughter, "…that the gods chose her to be with him, and yet they did not want him to have to forsake the immortal life or leave the brotherhood of the Phantom Fire. Do you, Falkor, choose to remain with the order and cleave to your eternal flame?"

"I do." He turned to the one woman he had waited thousands of years to claim and who now stood with her hands entwined with his. "Blood of my blood, will you bind yourself to me?"

"I will," she answered, her smile radiating warmth and happiness on this brand-new day at the dawn of a new era.

"Then it is done," said Zahran.

Danica Morris was feeling every single year of her life and every single day she'd spent as a member of the Seattle Police Department. There'd been a time, when she was young and hungry, when she had lived for the job. It had made her the youngest woman to ever make detective. But that laser focus on her career had cost her—friends, family, a fiancé, and time she would never get back. At almost thirty, she was exhausted and completely without a social life.

But tonight, she would see all of her hard work come to fruition. She was wrapping up a nearly year-long investigation into a cult-led trafficking operation.

Young people, mostly girls, were leaving home, joining the cult, and never being seen again.

At first, the bust had gone down like clockwork. Her team, along with the FBI, had moved in, surrounded the building, and burst into the warehouse, which was filled with cultists, victims in cages and enough paranormal paraphernalia to make New Orleans look normal.

"Good work, Detective Morris," said one of the FBI agents, whose advances she had been studiously ignoring for some time now.

"Thanks. I think with my team and yours, we've got this covered. I'll wait for CSI to get here and just make another sweep."

"I can stay and help," he said a little too eagerly.

"No. I've got this. But thanks for everything."

She turned away before she could see the disappointment in his eyes. He was a nice guy, but the last thing she needed was an affair gone wrong with a member of the Bureau. She began to move through the deserted warehouse—at least that's what the infrared readings showed—by herself, gun drawn. It never hurt to be careful.

Coming across a set of stairs that led down, she wondered where they could lead to or what their purpose might have been originally. Carefully, she opened the door and proceeded down. Unlike the cavernous but dry warehouse above, this place was dark, wet, and ominous. A kind of haunting sound came from up ahead. She rounded a stack of metal cages and then stopped.

Danica closed her eyes, shook her head, and then re-opened them. The noise stopped, leaving her staring into the darkest eyes of any creature she had ever seen.

Creature being the correct term.

For staring back at her, massive chains of iron pinning him to the floor, was a *dragon*. A real life, scaled and winged, mother-effing *dragon*.

"Holy crap," Danica murmured, her voice echoing in the chamber.

Slowly, painfully, he lifted his head. "Help me," he whispered, the voice of a man emerging from the dragon's mouth.

Now what was she supposed to do? Although it wasn't precisely the motto of the Seattle Police Department, weren't all cops supposed to serve and protect? How the hell was she supposed to do that with a dragon?

~

Warrick

His name was Warrick, and he was immortal—one of the fierce warriors of the Phantom Fire.

~

Curious about Warrick and the trouble he gets into? Click here to read Wild Fire.

A cop looking for the truth. A dragon looking for revenge. Can they work together to find justice?

Danica Morris had been a member of the Seattle Police Department for what felt like an eternity, but tonight, her hard work would finally pay off. She was wrapping up a nearly year-long investigation into a cult-led trafficking operation. Young people, mostly girls, were leaving home, joining the cult, and never being seen again.

The bust had gone down like clockwork. Moving through the deserted warehouse she found a set of stairs that led down. She heard a haunting sound coming from the depths of the building. Taking a deep breath, she descended a set of stairs and rounded a stack of metal cages. There, chained to the floor with heavy iron links, was a dragon. A real-life, scaled, and winged dragon.

Warrick, one of the Phantom Fire, had been chained and trapped in this cellar for a long time. Hearing someone approach he opens his eyes expecting his captors again. Only to find the most beautiful woman staring at him in shock, and he knew that she was his fated mate.

His captors were nowhere to be found, and as their eyes met Danica couldn't help but feel a strange connection between them. Despite her better judgment, she sets Warrick free and the two embark on a journey to uncover the truth and seek justice. But when they find themselves in the middle of a centuries-old battle between dragons and humans, will they be able to work together to find a solution?

BONUS SCENE

I have an **EXCLUSIVE** bonus scene as a thank you! All you have to do is click the link below, sign up for my newsletter, and you'll get an email giving you access!

SIGN UP HERE

Wild Fire

Dark Fire

Mystic River Shifters (small town shifter)

Defiant Mate

Savage Mate

Reckless Mate

Shameless Mate

Runaway Mate

Stolen Mate

Bah Humbug Mate

Hidden Mate

Unforeseen Mate

Shadow Mate

Book Set Vol. 1

Book Set Vol. 2

Book Set Vol. 3

Otter Cover Shifters (small town shifters/ spinoff Mystic River)

Suspicious Mate

Unexpected Mate

Substitute Mate

Accidental Mate

Feral Mate

Mystic Mate

Elusive Mate

Mysterious Mate

Syndicate Masters

Midwest

<u>Kiss of Luck</u>

<u>Stroke of Fortune</u>

<u>Twist of Fate</u>

Eastern Seaboard

<u>High Stakes</u>

<u>High Roller</u>

<u>High Bet</u>

La Cosa Nostra

<u>Ruthless Honor</u>

<u>Feral Oath</u>

<u>Defiant Vow</u>

Northern Lights

<u>Alliance</u>

<u>Complication</u>

<u>Judgment</u>

Syndicate Masters

<u>The Bargain</u>

<u>The Pact</u>

<u>The Agreement</u>

<u>The Understanding</u>

<u>The Pledge</u>

<u>Box Set</u>

Looking Glass Multiverse

<u>Shifted Reality</u>

<u>Shifted Existence</u>

<u>Shifted Dimension</u>

<u>Box Set</u>

Reign of Fire

<u>Dragon Storm</u>

<u>Dragon Roar</u>

<u>Dragon Fury</u>

Masters of Valor (spin off Masters of the Savoy)

<u>Prophecy</u>

<u>Illusion</u>

<u>Deception</u>

<u>Inheritance</u>

Masters of the Savoy

<u>Advance</u>

<u>Negotiation</u>

<u>Submission</u>

<u>Contract</u>

<u>Bound</u>

<u>Release</u>

Ghost Cat Canyon

<u>Determined</u>

<u>Untamed</u>

<u>Bold</u>

<u>Fearless</u>

<u>Strong</u>

Fated Legacy (spin-off Tangled Vines)

<u>Touch of Fate</u>

<u>Touch of Darkness</u>

<u>Touch of Light</u>

<u>Touch of Fire</u>

<u>Touch of Ice</u>

<u>Touch of Destiny</u>

Tangled Vines (spin-off Wayward Mates)

<u>Corked</u>

<u>Uncorked</u>

<u>Decanted</u>

<u>Breathe</u>

<u>Full Bodied</u>

<u>Late Harvest</u>

<u>Mulled Wine</u>

Wayward Mates

In Vino Veritas

Brought to Heel

Marked and Mated

Mastering His Mate

Taking His Mate

Claimed and Mated

Claimed and Mastered

Hunted and Claimed

Captured and Claimed

Wayward Mates Box Set One

Wayward Mates Box Set Two

Alpha Lords

Warlord

Overlord

Wolflord

Fated

Dragonlord

Contemporary Suspense

Club Tales (spinoff novellas Club series)

Tempting Alec

Enticing Kane

Captivating Nash

Club Series

Carriage House (spinoff Club Southside)

Viktor

Club Southside (spinoff Mercenary Masters)

<u>The Scoundrel</u>

<u>The Scavenger</u>

<u>The Rookie</u>

<u>The Sentinel</u>

<u>The Keeper</u>

<u>The Enforcer</u>

The Player

Mercenary Masters

<u>Devil Dog</u>

<u>Alpha Dog</u>

<u>Bull Dog</u>

<u>Top Dog</u>

<u>Big Dog</u>

<u>Sea Dog</u>

<u>Ice Dog</u>

Mystery, She Wrote

Invitation To Murder

<u>Murder Before Dawn</u>

<u>Hook, Line and Mystery</u>

<u>Paint Me A Murder</u>

Deadline To Murder

Relentless Pursuit (Duet)

To Love a Thief

My Fair Thief

Charade

Wild Mustang

Hampton

Mac

Croft

Noah

Thom

Reid

Crooked Creek Ranch

Taming His Cowgirl

Tamed on the Ranch

Co-writes

Masters of the Deep

Silent Predator

Fierce Predator

Savage Predator

Wicked Predator

Deadly Predator

ABOUT DELTA JAMES

Other books by Delta James: <u>https://www.deltajames.com/</u>

As a USA Today bestselling romance author, Delta James aims to captivate readers with stories about complex heroines and the dominant alpha males who adore them. For Delta, romance is more than just a love story; it's a journey with challenges and thrills along the way.

After creating a second chapter for herself that was dramatically different than the first, Delta now resides in Florida where she relaxes on warm summer evenings with her loveable pack of basset hounds as they watch the birds, squirrels and lizards. When not crafting fast-paced tales, she enjoys horseback riding, walks on the beach, and white-water rafting.

Her readers mean the world to her, and Delta tries to interact personally to as many messages as she can. If you'd like to chat or discuss books, you can find Delta on Instagram, Facebook, and in her private reader group https://www.facebook.com/groups/348982795738444.

Keep up with Delta on Social Media
[Facebook page](#)
[Facebook group](#)
[Instagram](#)
[TikTok](#)
[Bookbub](#)
[Goodreads](#)
[Patreon](#)

[Signup](#) for my newsletter and

Get the good stuff...
Each month Delta shares her writing updates, novel releases, exclusive content and some fun personal stories.
Plus - there's often a giveaway!

Thank you!

ACKNOWLEDGMENTS

Thank you to my Patreon supporters.
I couldn't do this without you!

Lori
Carol Chase
D F
Ellen
Tamara Crooks
Suzy Sawkins
Linda Kniffen-Wager
Karen Somerville